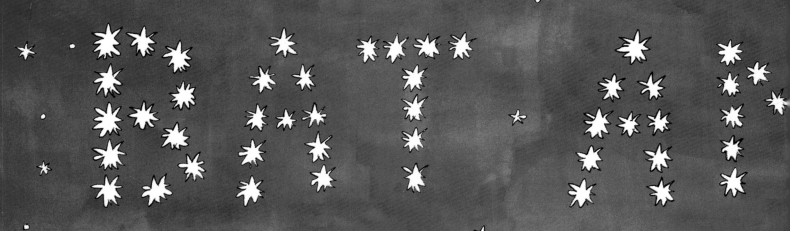

PITTER PATTER

by Patrick Jennings

illustrations by *Matthew Cordell*

ABRAMS BOOKS FOR YOUNG READERS

NEW YORK

Bat and Rat lived uptown, in the Hotel Midnight.

Bat's apartment was on the top floor, the thirty-third.

Rat's was in the basement.

They were best friends.

They were also a musical duo.

Bat wrote the music and played the piano.

RING! RING!

One night, Rat's phone rang.
"Hello?" she said.

"Hi, Rat," Bat said. "Are you
ready for our gig tonight?"

"As a matter of fact, I'm not," Rat answered. "I'm still working on your wonderful new tune. I want the song to be about things I like, but I can't seem to get the words right."

"Is ice cream one of the things you like?" Bat asked. "It's so hot tonight."

Rat smiled. "I'll meet you in the lobby!"

"Yay!" Bat said.

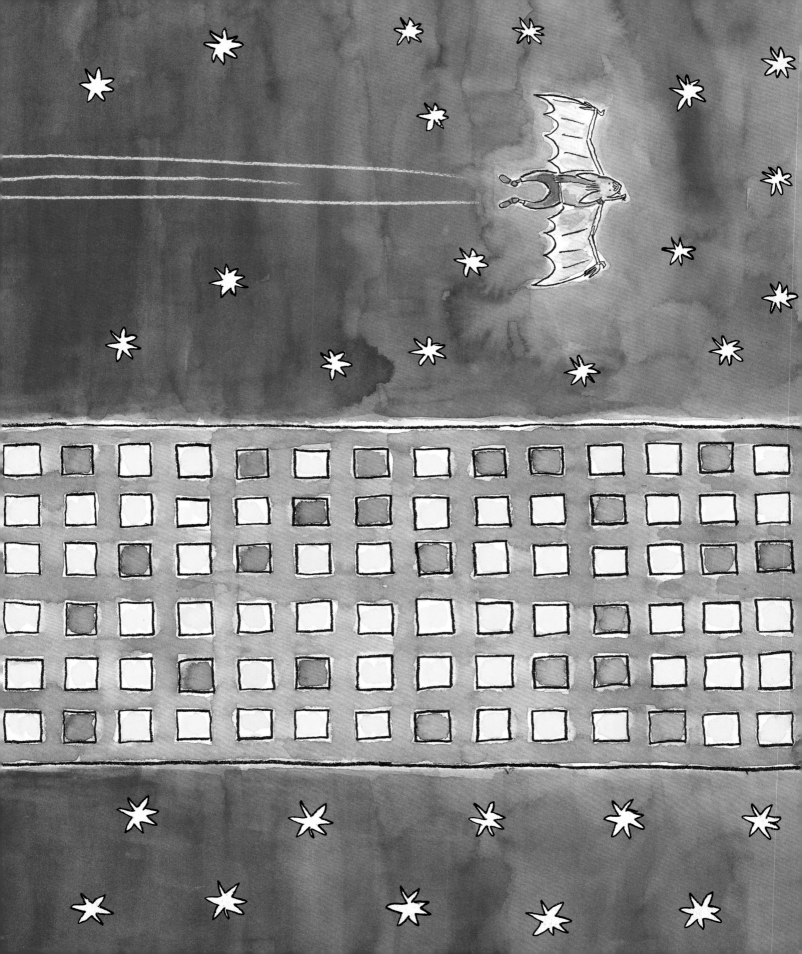

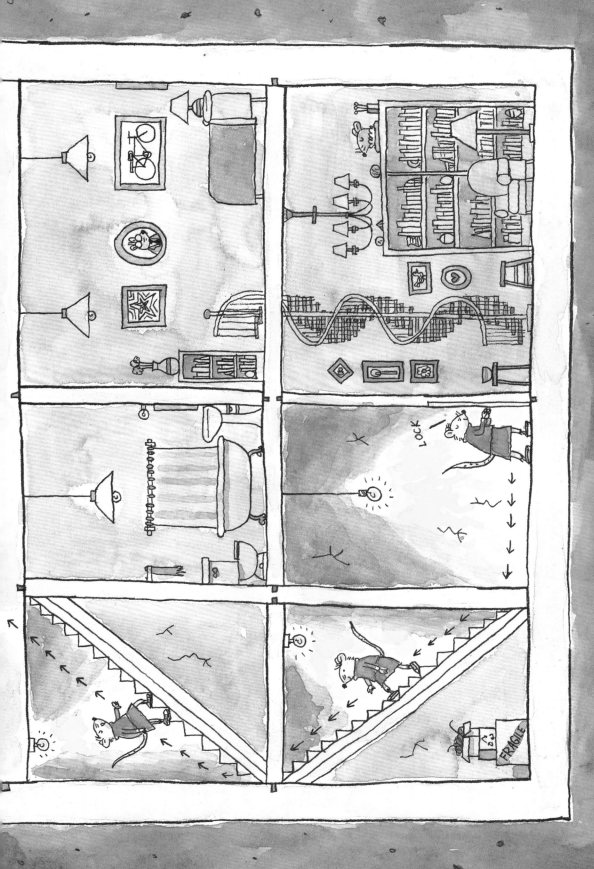

"Here we are!" said Bat. "Ice cream!"

"Mosquito Ripple!" Bat squealed. "That's my favorite flavor! But, oh—Butter Beetle Pecan! That's my favorite, too!"

"I can't possibly decide,"
Bat said.

"They have Mint Fly Chip tonight,"
Rat said. "Isn't that your favorite?"

Bat frowned. "I wish you had not
told me that! Now there are
THREE favorites I want!"

"Bat, I would like to treat you to a
triple scoop tonight," Rat said.

"You would? Oh, Rat, I love you,"
said Bat.

"Ditto," said Rat.

"Oh, no!" Bat said. "That's Tutti-Frutti! *Tutti-Frutti* is my favorite!"

"So what will it be tonight, Bat and Rat?" the ice cream scooper asked.

Rat said, "I'll have a scoop of Gorgonzola Swirl on a plain cone, please. And Bat can have whatever he likes. My treat."

Bat took a deep breath and then said, "I want Mint Fly
Chip . . . and Mosquito Ripple . . . and Butter Beetle
Pecan . . . and Tutti-Frutti . . . and . . ."

"Rat, can you hold my cone so I can fly up
and lick my top scoop?"

"Of course," Rat said.

"Dee-lish!" Bat said.

Just then, a young hare
zipped by on her skateboard.

"Rat!" Bat shouted.
"It's teetering!"

Rat tried to keep the
tower of ice cream
balanced . . .

. . . but it toppled anyway.
Into the gutter.

Then a bus
zoomed by.

"NO!" Bat screeched. "Oh, Rat! You are so bumbly! You are so, so BUTTERFINGERY!"

"What I am is so, so sorry," Rat said.

Bat saw Rat's so, so sorry face. "I guess it's not your fault, Rat. I'm sorry I screeched at you."

"That's okay," Rat said. "Look. Now we each have one scoop."

"You know," Bat said with a sigh, "Mint Fly Chip is my *favorite* favorite."

"Oh, Bat!" Rat cried. "That's it!"

"That's what?" Bat asked, confused.

"The words I needed for my song! Thank you, Bat!"

"You're welcome," said Bat.

That night at the Twelve O'Clock Room . . .

"For our next number," Rat said, "we would like to play you a brand-new song. The words were inspired by Bat. It's called 'Favorite Favorite.'"

Bat tickled an intro on the piano. Then Rat began to sing:

That thing you love . . . you must savor it.
Nothing above . . . it's your favorite.

And favorite means it's at the very top.
So very high you must not let it . . .

. . . drop.

My favorite cheese is runny and smelly.

My favorite noodle is vermicelli.

My favorite headwear's a porkpie hat.
But my favorite favorite is Bat.

My favorite dinner?
A rotten egg roll.
My favorite singer?
Rat King Cole.

My favorite home is
a basement flat.
But my favorite favorite
is Bat.

I said my favorite favorite . . .
My very favorite favorite . . .
My FAVORITE favorite favorite is . . .
My . . .
         . . . friend . . .
                    . . . B-A-A-A-A-A-A-A-T!

"Thank you. Thank you so much," Rat said to the crowd. "We're going to take a short break now, but don't go away. We'll be back before you know it."

"I love you!" Bat yelled to the audience.

"Ditto!" said Rat.

The illustrations in this book were made
with pencil and watercolor on paper.

Cataloging in Publication Data has been applied for and may be
obtained from the Library of Congress.

ISBN: 978-1-4197-0160-3

Text copyright © 2012 Patrick Jennings
Illustrations copyright © 2012 Matthew Cordell

Book design by Chad W. Beckerman

Printed and bound in China
10 9 8 7 6 5 4 3 2 1

Abrams Books for Young Readers are available at special discounts
when purchased in quantity for premiums and promotions as well as
fundraising or educational use. Special editions can also be created to
specification. For details, contact specialsales@abramsbooks.com or
the address below.

ABRAMS
THE ART OF BOOKS SINCE 1949
115 West 18th Street
New York, NY 10011
www.abramsbooks.com

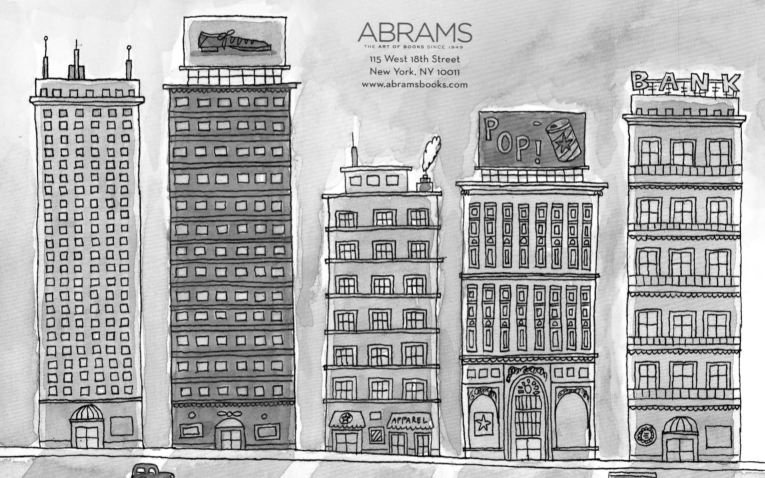

To that fabulous duo,
Paige & Maya!
—P.J.
To Rosemary Stimola
—M.C.

A Gift for

_____

Presented by

_____

Y
OU
KNOW
YOU'RE OVER
THE HILL WHEN...

Y

OU

KNOW

YOU'RE OVER

THE HILL WHEN...

A HUMOROUS
COLLECTION FOR
THE YOUNG AT HEART

SHELLEY KLEIN

The Reader's Digest Association, Inc.
Pleasantville, NY / Montreal

First published as *You Know You're Past It When...* in Great Britain in 2008
by Michael O'Mara Books Limited:
9 Lion Yard
Tremadoc Road
London SW4 7NQ

FOR READER'S DIGEST
U.S. Project Editor: Siobhan Sullivan
Project Production Coordinator: Wayne Morrison
Editorial Consultant: Nancy Shuker
Senior Art Director: George McKeon
Executive Editor, Trade Publishing: Dolores York
Manufacturing Manager: Elizabeth Dinda
Vice President, U.S. Operations: Michael Braunschweiger
Associate Publisher: Rosanne McManus
President and Publisher, Trade Publishing: Harold Clarke

Library of Congress Cataloging-in-Publication Data

Klein, Shelley.
You know you're over the hill when-- : a humorous collection for the young
at heart / [compiled by] Shelley Klein.
    p. cm.
Previously published in Britain in 2008 under the title: You know you're past
it when--
    ISBN 978-1-60652-025-3
    1. Aging--Humor. 2. Old age--Humor. 3. Older people--Humor. I. Title.
PN6231.A43K59 2009
818'.602--dc22

                                                              2009006372

We are committed to both the quality of our products and the service we provide to our customers. We value your comments, so please feel free to contact us.

The Reader's Digest Association, Inc.
Adult Trade Publishing
Reader's Digest Road
Pleasantville, NY 10570-7000

For more Reader's Digest products and information, visit our website:
www.rd.com (in the United States)
www.readersdigest.ca (in Canada)

Printed in the United States of America

1 3 5 7 9 10 8 6 4 2

Introduction

The only real antidote to aging—other than Botox injections—is a sense of humor. As Groucho Marx, that great doctor of comedy who lived to be 87, famously said, "A laugh is like an aspirin, only it works twice as fast." Following that vein, *You Know You're Over the Hill When…* is a collection of anecdotes, stories, and jokes that poke fun at the great inevitability—growing older.

Chances are you will recognize yourself in some of the stories in this book, and we hope they will give you a chuckle. We also hope it will make you feel better to know that you are not alone in facing the loss of your hearing, your eye sight, and the name of your best friend. It was Bette Davis who said, "Growing old is not for sissies." That was some years ago, and despite the miracles of modern medicine and such common spare parts as knees, hips, and shoulders, she wasn't wrong.

If these stories make you laugh, know that you are not only aging gracefully, but enjoying life. "Age is an issue of mind over matter," said Mark Twain. "If you don't mind, it doesn't matter."

The foibles of growing older fill many categories. We have chosen twelve. "Wise Words…or Wise Cracks" includes some of the pearls of senior wisdom that sometimes backfire on us. "Tricks of the Trade" illustrates some of the tricks we learn along the way to cope with aging. "Oooh La La" concentrates on the continuing battle of the sexes, which never seems to run out of steam. "The Doctor Is In" covers the health issues that chase us through the ages. "Triumph...or Tragedy" gives us hope for our continuing effectiveness despite frequent set-backs. "Thanks for the Memory" implies that we have some great ones, which we do, but that we can't always call on them at will.

"Life's Little Slips" exemplifies just that: things that don't come out quite the way we expected them to. "How Shall We Celebrate" reminds us that there will always be occasions for fun. "Vanity Not So Fair" broaches some of the difficulties of keeping a la mode forever. "Frankly, My Dear" takes an honest look at some of our less tactful imperfections in advancing age. "And So It Goes. . ." suggests that at a certain point, we are not always masters of our fate. "Good-bye and Amen" is just that.

George Burns, who certainly was a model for staying young at heart a long time—he died at age 100—admonished, "You can't help getting older, but you don't have to be old." Laughing keeps you young at heart.

—The Editors

Table of Contents

1

Wise Words...
or Wise Cracks?

YOU KNOW YOU'RE OVER THE HILL WHEN...

- You can live without sex, but not without your glasses.

- Happy hour is a nap in the afternoon.

- You have all the time in the world to put your snapshots in photo albums, but you have no idea who the people in the photos are.

- Your children are beginning to look middle-aged.

- You keep more food than beer in the fridge.

- You're asleep, but others worry that you're dead.

- You and your teeth don't sleep together.

- Your ears are hairier than your head.

AMAZING

One day, the octogenarian Austrian economist Ludwig von Mises was asked how he felt getting up each morning.

His reply?

"Amazed!"

GOOD PUT-DOWN

You know for sure you're entering your golden years when everyone around you starts to look (and generally is) younger than you. Policemen seem to be about fifteen years old and doctors about twelve, so imagine the Hollywood director Billy Wilder's consternation when he was summoned to the office of the "movie brat" who had taken over the studio.

"Great to meet you at last, Billy," the youngster is supposed to have said. "Hope you'll come on the team. Believe we can make you some very interesting offers. Now, Billy, tell me—what have you done?"

Wilder is said to have paused a second and then replied politely: "After you..."

GOOD HAIR DAY

Two ladies sat on a bench, talking.

One said to the other, "Good heavens! Who did your hair? It looks like a wig!"

The second lady replied, "It is a wig."

"Really?" pondered the first woman. "You could never tell!"

WHAT A BOTHER

French actor Maurice Chevalier and U.S. comedian Phil Silvers were chatting backstage one evening during a show, when a group of lovely young women passed by.

Chevalier sighed longingly. "Ah," he remarked, "if only I were twenty years older."

"Don't you mean twenty years younger?" Silvers asked.

"No, if I were twenty years older," Chevalier replied, "these girls would not bother me the way they do!"

DECAYED TENEMENTS

In 1826, former President John Adams died.

Describing his last meeting with Adams, his friend Daniel Webster said: "Someone, a friend of his, came in and made particular inquiry of his health. Adams answered, 'I inhabit a weak, frail, decayed tenement battered by the winds and broken in upon by the storms, and, from all I can learn, the landlord does not intend to repair!'"

FROM SHOW-BIZ TO NO-BIZ

No industry is more cruel to those no longer in the flush of youth than show business. As the acid-tongued Cher observed, "In this business it takes time to be really good— and by that time, you're obsolete."

OBSERVATIONS ON OLD AGE

In the TV show *3rd Rock from the Sun*, written by Andy Cowan, the characters provide these insights into aging:

Mary: When men get gray hair, they look distinguished. When women get gray hair, they look old.
Dick: When women get breasts, they look sexy. When men get breasts, they look old.

TOILET BREAKS

The author John Mortimer certainly knows all about the trials and tribulations of growing old, for as he once said, "When you get to my age, life seems little more than one long march to and from the lavatory."

CHANGING TIMES

The aging actor John Barrymore was once asked by a young newspaper reporter whether acting still gave him as much pleasure as it had in his early career.

"Young man, I am seventy-five," Barrymore replied. "Nothing is as much fun as it used to be!"

SHHH!

Knowing you're over the hill is not something you necessarily want the world to know about, or those of a darker persuasion, as this quotation from Nicholas Chamfort, which is reproduced in *The Oxford Book of Ages*, attests.

"A woman of ninety said to M. de Fontenelle, when he was ninety-five: 'Death has forgotten us.'

"'Shhh!' de Fontenelle answered, putting his finger over his mouth."

HATS OFF

A lady in her forties walked into a milliner's to try on a hat. The sales assistant fawned over her, declaring, "You look wonderful in that hat. Really, it makes you look ten years younger when you wear it."

"Then I don't want it," exclaimed the customer. "I can't afford to put on ten years every time I take my hat off!"

KEY TEST

If you forget where you put your car keys, that's normal. If you don't know what to do with them when you find them, you might be a senior.

DAMNED CRICKETS

When Mel Brooks was asked by an interviewer what he thought of critics, apparently he misheard the question, for he is said to have replied: "They're very noisy at night. You can't sleep in the country because of them."

It was only when the interviewer explained that he had asked about critics not crickets that Brooks corrected the mistake and said: "Oh, *critics*! What good are they? They can't make music with their hind legs."

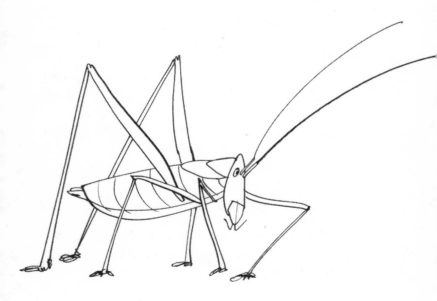

TURN ME ON, TOM!

One afternoon in the Georgia Statehouse, representative Anne Mueller explained to House Speaker Tom Murphy that her microphone had been switched off.

"Mr. Speaker, will you please turn me on?" she requested.

"Thirty years ago," replied Murphy, "I would have tried!"

IN IT FOR THE LONG HAUL

How do you account for your longevity?" asked the reporter on Harvey's 110th birthday.

"You might call me a health nut," Harvey replied. "I never smoked. I never drank. I was always in bed and sound asleep by 10 o'clock. And I've always walked three miles a day, rain or shine."

"But," said the reporter, "I had an uncle who followed that exact routine and died when he was 62. How come it didn't work for him?"

"All I can say," replied Harvey, "is that he didn't keep it up long enough."

—*Lutheran Digest*

WHY NOW?

The judge was trying to change the mind of a woman filing for divorce. "You're 92," he said. "Your husband's 94. You've been married for 73 years. Why give up now?"

"Our marriage has been on the rocks for quite a while," the woman explained, "but we decided to wait until the children died."

—Joyce Brothers

BABY BADGES

English music-hall performer Seymour Hicks definitely knew a thing or two about the signs of being over the hill when he commented: "You will recognize, my boy, the first sign of old age: it is when you go out into the streets of London and realize for the first time how young the policemen look."

A NEW YOU

Bill Cosby obviously knows all about that special era termed one's golden years. Take, for example, the following observation.

"I am having to learn to accept a new me; one who dials a telephone number and, while the phone is ringing, forgets whom he is calling."

GOOD POINT, MR. MORTIMER

It's not pleasant growing old and feeling as if the world has left you behind, but at least John Mortimer has found one positive thing to be said for entering the autumn of one's life.

"Just imagine," he says, "what life would be like if you could recite every word of Britney Spears's latest hit."

PICTURE PERFECT

I had been thinking about coloring my hair. One day while going through a magazine, I came across an ad for a hair-coloring product featuring a beautiful young model with hair a shade that I liked. Wanting a second opinion, I asked my husband, "How do you think this color would look on a face with a few wrinkles?"

He looked at the picture, crumpled it up, straightened it out and studied it again. "Just great, hon."

—Joan Keyser

NO TIME TO WAIT

Because they had no reservations at a busy restaurant, my elderly neighbor and his wife were told there would be a 45-minute wait for a table.

"Young man, we're both 90 years old," he told the maitre d'. "We may not have 45 minutes."

They were seated immediately.

—Rita Kalish

SELF-ACCEPTANCE

Learn to enjoy your own company. You are the one person you can count on living with for the rest of your life.

—Ann Richards in *O: The Oprah Magazine*

RETIREMENT

For over 40 years my grandfather put in long hours at his job, so I was more than a little curious about the way he filled his days since his retirement.

"How has life changed?" I asked.

A man of few words, he replied, "Well I get up in the morning with nothing to do, and I go to bed at night with it half-done."

—Dennis Lundberg

GENERATION GAP

Korey, my granddaughter, came to spend a few weeks with me, and I decided to teach her how to sew. After I had gone through a lengthy demonstration of how to thread the machine, Korey stepped back and put her hands on her hips. "You mean you can do all that," she said in disbelief, "but you can't operate my Game Boy?"

—Nell Baron

CO-ED CATCH

Heading off to college at the age of 40, I was a bit self-conscious about my advancing years. One morning I complained to my husband that I was the oldest student in my class.

"Even the teacher is younger than I am," I said.

"Yeah, but look at it from my point of view," he said optimistically. "I thought my days of fooling around with college girls were over."

—Brenda McMillen

A BIG OPINION

Having fought the battle of the bulge most of my life, I found the battle getting even harder as I approached middle age. One evening, after trying on slacks that were too tight, I said to my husband, "I'll be so glad when we become grandparents. After all, who cares if grandmothers are fat?"

His prompt reply: "Grandfathers."

—Iris Cavin

A SAPPY SENTIMENT

Paul was in his mid-60s and had just retired. He was planning to landscape his yard and was trying to find some small shrubs or trees. Burleigh, a 90-year-old from across the street, offered Paul some white-ash saplings that were about two feet tall.

Paul asked, "How long will it take them to be full grown?"

"Twenty years or so," replied Burleigh.

"No good for me, then," said Paul. "I won't be around that long."

The 90-year-old shook his head and replied, "We'll miss ya!"

—Clydene Savage

2

Tricks
of the Trade

YOU KNOW YOU'RE OVER THE HILL WHEN...

- You're on the floor cleaning or playing with the kids when the phone rings, and it's just easier to crawl to the phone than to get up and walk there.

- Your friends compliment you on your new alligator shoes... but you're barefoot.

- You're given one of those books about the "joys of aging" as a present (such as this one).　　　—Garrison Keillor

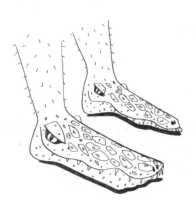

- You turn out the light for economic reasons instead of romantic ones.   —Herbert J. Karet

- Your doctor doesn't give you X-rays any more, but just holds you up to the light.

- You tell your friends you're having an affair and they ask, "Are you having it catered?"

- A sexy babe catches your fancy—and your pacemaker opens the garage door nearest you.

- You're young at heart, but a lot older in other places.

GOOD TIP

I was with my husband at a baseball game in Boston's Fenway Park when I decided to go get myself a hot dog. As I stood up my husband asked me to buy him a beer. The young clerk at the concession stand asked to see verification of age.

"You've got to be kidding," I said. "I'm almost 40 years old."

He apologized, but said he had to insist. When I showed him my license, the clerk served me the beer. "That will be $4.25."

I gave him $5 and told him to keep the change. "The tip's for carding me," I said.

He put the change in the tip cup. "Thanks," he said. "Works every time."

—Angie Dewhurst

HOT FLUSH

It was a hot sunny day as Caroline left the plumbing supply house, and several young workmen were sitting around shirtless. To match the weather, Caroline herself was wearing a shorter skirt than usual, revealing a shapely pair of legs for someone in her late forties. She was aware of the workmen as she walked to her car, but was taken completely by surprise when she heard a male voice call out, "Can I have your phone number?"

Caroline blushed slightly. What would her husband say? It was years since she had been propositioned and she was flattered by the attention. But she continued walking toward her car, albeit with an extra wiggle of her bottom.

Then the shout came again: "Please can I have your phone number?"

Her mind was now racing to guess which of the workmen was her admirer; was it the Brad Pitt look-alike with the tanned body or the dark-haired one with the tattoos? Either way, it had made her day.

Still determined not to turn around, she self-consciously adjusted the hem of her skirt before delving into her bag for her car keys. She was just about to unlock the car when the voice shouted for a third time, more urgently than before: "Please can I have your phone number?"

It was time for the ice maiden to melt: to hell with the boring husband and the three kids; she wanted some excitement in her life and turned to see which young stud found her irresistible.

The workmen were indeed staring at her, as was a bald-headed man in his sixties, breathlessly clutching a piece of paper.

"Please can I have your phone number, Mrs. McLean," he shouted, "or I won't be able to let you know when we can deliver your new toilet bowl."

BEATING FAST

Toward the end of her life, the actress Sarah Bernhardt lived in a top-floor apartment in Paris. One day, a fan paid her a call, but became very out of breath from climbing so many steps to get there.

"*Madame*," he said, "why do you live so high up?"

"My dear friend," Bernhardt replied, "it is the only way I can still make the hearts of men beat faster."

GETTING HEALTHIER

Two guys were playing poker, talking, when the subject turned to getting older. The first guy said, "Women have all the luck when it comes to growing old."

"What do you mean?" asked the second guy.

"Well," replied the first, "I can't recall the last time I was able to get it up in bed, but my wife is healthier than ever."

"Healthier? How do you mean?" his buddy wondered aloud.

"Years ago, when we were younger, every night before bed she'd get these terrible headaches," his friend replied. "But now that we're older, she hasn't had a headache in years."

NEW TRICKS, OLD DOGS

During an appearance on Conan O'Brien's TV show comedian Tracy Morgan revealed how all of his friends were trying to become rap artists, including his forty-one-year-old brother.

"What's *he* rapping about?" Conan quickly joked. "Lower back pain?"

SEAT, SIR?

The older one grows, the more one needs to sit down, as comic George Burns knew only too well.

Even in his golden years, he was still to be found performing two-hour shows. However, he explained, "I do ten minutes standing up and fifty minutes sitting in a chair."

DON'T ASK MY AGE

One day, the census surveyor was doing his rounds. He knocked on Miss Campbell's door. Miss Campbell happily answered all his questions—except one. She wouldn't tell the census man her age.

"Miss Campbell, everyone tells me their age," he said kindly.

"What? Did Miss Elizabeth Hill and Miss Katie Hill tell you theirs?"

"Yes."

"Well, I'm the same age as them," confided Miss Campbell.

So the census taker wrote down: "As old as the Hills."

MISTAKEN IDENTITY

One day, the American writer and comedian Robert Benchley was out to dinner with his son Nathaniel.

"We went to the Trocadero," writes Nathaniel in his memoir of his father, *Robert Benchley: A Biography*. "When, in the course of events, we left to go home, he went to a uniformed man at the door and said, 'Would you get us a taxi, please?'

"The man turned round and regarded him icily. 'I'm very sorry,' he said. 'I happen to be a rear admiral in the United States Navy.'

"'All right, then,' said my father. 'Get us a battleship.'"

LITTLE WHITE LIES...

One day, Archie rushes in to see his GP.

"Doctor, you *have* to prescribe me something to make me feel young again. I've got a date with a gorgeous woman this evening and I'm in urgent need of a pep-me-up."

His doctor looks at Archie for a long time, and then says honestly, "Archie, you're in your eighties—there's not a great deal I can do for you."

"But, Doctor," replies Archie, "my friend Reg is much older than I am and he says he makes love to his girlfriend five or six times a week."

"OK," says the doctor, "so you can say it too!"

GETTING THE SNIP

One of the clearest signs of aging for men is when their libido drops or, worse still, when they become impotent.

Such was obviously the case for Irish poet W. B. Yeats, who at the age of sixty-nine not only suffered from this condition in the bedroom, but also thought it prevented him from producing new work.

Fed up with this state of affairs, he decided to undergo an operation developed by Austrian doctor Eugen Steinach (1861–1944), which was in effect a vasectomy, because in those days people believed that a vasectomy would increase one's testosterone levels and subsequently one's virility.

Naturally, the operation didn't work—but Yeats did feel rejuvenated enough to pick up his pen again, so at least some good came of it!

GARAGE GRASS

Talk about being over the hill... A woman by the name of Amy Brasher was apparently arrested in San Antonio, Texas, on drug charges after a mechanic reported to the police that he had found eighteen packets of marijuana stuffed into the engine of the car that Ms. Brasher had brought in to his garage for an oil check.

According to Ms. Brasher, she hadn't realized that the mechanic would need to lift the hood of the car in order to carry out the job.

THE OLDER YOU GROW,
THE MORE WILY YOU GET

A hotshot New York lawyer in his twenties went grouse shooting in rural Tennessee. He shot and killed a bird, but it fell into a farmer's field on the other side of a fence. As the lawyer climbed over the fence, the farmer drove up on his tractor and asked him what he was doing.

The lawyer replied, "I shot a grouse and it fell into this field, and now I'm going to pick it up."

The farmer, drawing on his years of experience, replied, "This is my property, and you are not coming over here."

The lawyer said, "I am one of the best attorneys in the U.S. and if you don't let me get that game bird, I'll sue you and take everything you own."

The farmer grinned and said, "Apparently, you don't know how we do things here in Tennessee. We settle small disagreements like this with the Tennessee Three-Kick Rule."

"What is the Tennessee Three-Kick Rule?" asked the lawyer.

The farmer replied, "Well, first I kick you three times and then you kick me three times, and so on, back and forth, until someone gives up."

The attorney thought about the proposed contest and decided that he could easily take the old man down, so he agreed that the contest should go ahead.

The farmer slowly climbed down from the tractor and walked up to the city boy. His first kick planted the toe of his heavy boot into the lawyer's groin and dropped him to his knees. His second kick nearly broke the man's nose. The lawyer was flat on his belly when the farmer's third kick to a kidney nearly caused him to quit.

However, he summoned every bit of his will and managed to get to his feet and said, "OK, enough! Now it's my turn."

The old farmer smiled and said, "No, I give up, you can have the grouse."

HEAD IN THE CLOUDS

Plenty of us know we're over the hill when our looks begin to fade and our bodies begin to crumble or wizen or both, but for some people, it's when the simple things in life start to become really puzzling.

Hastings Randall, who was a moral philosopher and theologian at New College, Oxford in the early twentieth century, was one day found by an undergraduate pumping up the front wheel of his bicycle. Said the student to Randall, "Excuse me, sir, but that will do no good."

Hastings Randall asked why.

"Because it's your back tire that is flat," replied the student.

"Goodness me," said Randall, "do you mean to tell me they're not connected?"

TO EAT OR NOT TO EAT

The Nobel Prize-winning chemist Harold Urey (1893–1981), who was famed for his forgetfulness, was stopped in the street by a friend of his one sunny afternoon. After a brief conversation, the men began to go their separate ways—

until, that is, Urey turned round and asked: "John, which way was I walking when I met you?"

His friend pointed in the right direction.

"Oh good," said Urey, "that means I've already had my lunch!"

DON'T MESS WITH ME, SONNY

A property tycoon was backing his Bentley into the last available parking space when a zippy blue convertible whipped in behind him to take the spot. The twenty-something driver leaped out and said, "Sorry, Pops, but you've got to be young and smart to do that."

The tycoon paid no attention to the remark and simply kept reversing until his Bentley had crushed the sports car into a crumpled heap.

"Sorry, son, you've got to be old and rich to do that!"

LONG MARRIAGES

Getting irritated with your spouse is par for the course, but you really know you're getting on in life when you start telling others just how irritating your partner can be.

Such was the case when the actress Shirley Maclaine asked Samuel Goldwyn's wife, Frances, what it was like being married to the same man for more than thirty-five years.

"It gets worse every day," replied Mrs. Goldwyn. "Thirty-five years ago, I told Sam to come home and I'd fix him lunch. He's been coming home for lunch every day for thirty-five years!"

GOOD OLD GEORGE

When George Clooney was twenty-one years old, he worked as a chauffeur for his late Aunt Rosemary [Clooney] when she was a singer in the 4 Girls 4 with Martha Raye, Kay Starr and Helen O'Connell.

He recalls Raye making him stop the car so she could, as Clooney explained, "just stick out her leg to take a leak on the side of the road. Aunt Rosemary would say: 'Don't turn around, George, or you'll learn too much about the aging process!'"

CHECK THIS OUT

There was an ailing man who was a real miser. Just before he died, he said to his wife, "When I die, I want you to take all my money and put it in the coffin. I want to take my money to the afterlife with me." And so he got his wife to swear to him, on her mother's grave, that when he passed away, she would put all of his money in his coffin with him.

Well, he eventually died. He was stretched out in the casket, his wife sitting beside him, dressed in black, and her friend sitting next to her. After they'd finished the ceremony, and just before the undertakers got ready to close the coffin, the wife said, "Wait! Just a moment."

She had a brown envelope with her, which she placed firmly in the coffin. Then the undertakers locked the coffin and rolled it away.

The wife's friend said, "I know you were not stupid enough to put all that money in there with your husband."

The loyal spouse replied, "Listen, I'm a Christian; I cannot go back on my word. I promised him that I was going to put that money into the casket with him."

"You mean to tell me you put that money in there?"

"I surely did," said the wife. "I got it altogether, put it into my account, and wrote him a check. If he can cash it, he can spend it."

MARIANNE MOORE'S FLYING CIRCUS

A young man arrived at the home of poet Marianne Moore with a stack of books for her to sign. Glancing round the room, the young man admired the bookcases and ornaments, until finally his eyes came to rest on what looked like some sort of medieval contraption hanging by two chains from the door frame.

Marianne Moore was at this time in her seventies, so it seemed impertinent to ask her what it was; nonetheless, the young man plucked up his courage.

"Miss Moore, what is that up there in the doorway?" he said.

Without looking up, she replied, "Oh, that's my trapeze."

I'M STILL STANDING... OR AM I?

Despite having reached seventy years of age, actor Burt Reynolds was determined to do all his own stunts on the set of the 1998 thriller *Crazy Six*.

"Look, I can do this. I can still fall," he told the film's producers. "I just can't get up."

DIZZY BLONDE

How lovely you look, my dear!" gushed a wedding guest to the bride. And then she whispered, "Whatever happened to that dizzy blonde your groom used to date?"

"I dyed my hair," replied the bride.

—Kevin Benningfield
in Louisville, Ky., Courier-Journal

OLDER AND MUCH WISER

Sometimes, fun can be had with the younger generation when it comes to being over the hill. Who among us has not teased and tormented youngsters with our hard-won knowledge and oh-so-improved capacity for pulling their legs? The following story amply demonstrates the mischievous side of being senior.

One afternoon, a young man, who was an avid golfer, found himself with a couple of hours at his disposal. He quickly came to the conclusion that if he hurried and played very fast, he could squeeze in nine holes on the fairways before he had to attend a business dinner.

Just as he was about to tee off, an old-timer hobbled over and asked if he could accompany the young man as he was golfing alone. Not able to refuse the request, he allowed the old gent to join him.

To his surprise, the man played reasonably well. He didn't hit the ball far, but he pottered along steadily and didn't waste time.

They reached the ninth fairway, and the young man found himself with a tough shot. There was a large oak tree right in front of him, directly between his ball and the green.

He considered how to take the shot for a good long while. Then the young man heard the old man mutter, "You know, when I was your age, I'd hit the ball right over that tree."

With that challenge placed before him, the youngster swung hard and hit the ball right smack into the top of the tree trunk, from where it thudded back on the ground, not an inch from where it had been originally.

The old man offered one more comment: "Of course, when I was your age, that oak tree was only three feet tall."

SPEEDING SENIORS

A police officer spots a car traveling at just 20 m.p.h. He thinks to himself, "This tortoise is just as dangerous as the speeding hare!" So he switches on his siren and pulls the driver over.

Approaching the vehicle, he notes that there are four mature ladies inside—two in the front and two in the back—wide-eyed and each of them as white as a sheet.

The driver, clearly bewildered, says to him, "Officer, I don't understand, I was doing exactly the speed limit! What seems to be the problem?"

"Ma'am," the officer replies, "you weren't speeding, but you should know that driving slower than the speed limit can also be a hazard to other road users."

"Slower than the speed limit? No, sir, I was doing the speed limit exactly... Twenty miles an hour!" the old woman says proudly.

The police officer, trying to stifle a guffaw, explains to her that "20" is the route number, not the speed limit.

A bit shamefaced, the woman smiles and thanks the officer for highlighting her mistake.

"Before I let you go, ma'am," he says, "I have to ask— is everyone in this vehicle all right? These women seem awfully quiet and they're looking rather peaky."

"Oh, they'll be OK in a few moments, sir. We just got off Route 118."

HONEYMOON

"John, I can see that all your buttons are sewed on perfectly. You must be married!"

"That's right. Sewing on buttons was the first thing my wife taught me on our honeymoon."

—Chayan

IF ONLY YOU KNEW

A woman on the wrong side of sixty gets on to a packed bus and stands directly in front of a seated young man. Holding her hand to her chest, she says to the chap, "If you knew what I have, you would give me your seat." The man gets up and gives his seat to the lady.

It's a hot day on the bus. The girl sitting next to the woman takes out a fan and starts fanning herself. The lady looks up and says, "If you knew what I have, you would give me that fan." The girl, concerned, immediately hands over her fan.

Twenty minutes later, the woman gets up and says to the bus driver, "Halt! I want to get off here." The bus driver tells her he has to drop her at the next bus stop; he can't just pull up in the middle of the road. With her hand across her chest, she tells the driver, "If you knew what I have, you would let me off the bus right here."

The bus driver applies the brakes and opens the door to let her out. As she's walking off the bus, he asks, "Madam, what is it you have?"

The wily woman looks at him and nonchalantly replies, "Chutzpah."

EGGS

A man was asked by his wife to pick up a bra for her. She told him the correct size and color, and sent him on his way. By the time he arrived at the shop, however, he had forgotten everything his wife had told him.

A kindly assistant tried to help him out. "Is she the size of a melon?"

"No, smaller."

"A grapefruit?"

"No, smaller."

"An egg?"

"Yes," shouted the old man. "Fried!"

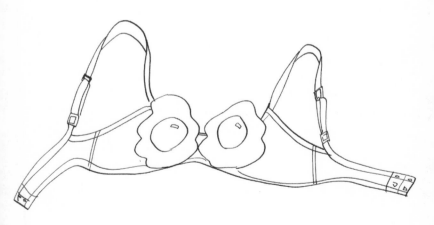

HOW SWEET

A little girl asked her mother for ten cents to give to an old lady in the park. Her mother was touched by the child's kindness and gave her the required sum.

"There you are, my dear," said the mother. "But, tell me, isn't the lady able to work any more?"

"Oh yes," came the reply. "She sells sweets."

—Harillon and Suzanne LeClercq

TURN A BLIND EYE

The key to successful aging is to pay as little attention to it as possible.

—Judith Regan in More

3

Ooooh la la!

YOU KNOW YOU'RE OVER THE HILL WHEN...

- Your other half says, "Let's go upstairs and make love," and you answer, "Darling, I can't do both!"

- You start getting symptoms in the places you used to get urges.
  —Denis Norden

- Going braless pulls all the wrinkles out of your face.

- Your idea of a workout is getting into your bra every morning.

- It takes two tries to get up from the couch.

- You have two pairs of spectacles, one of which you use to locate the other.

- Your joints are more accurate than the National Weather Service.

- You don't remember when your wild oats turned to prunes and porridge.

- Getting lucky means you find your car in the parking lot.

LOWER, LOWER

A frustrated man goes to see his GP.

"Doc, I want my sex drive lowered."

"Now, now," answered the doctor, "you're getting on a bit these days. Don't you think your libido is all in your head?"

"You're damned right it is!" replied the man. "That's why I want it lowered!"

BAD SEX

A middle-aged man was having an annual physical. As the doctor was listening to his heart with the stethoscope, the medic exclaimed, "Oh, no!"

In a panic, the man asked the doctor what the problem was.

"Well," said the physician, "you have a bad heart murmur. Do you smoke?"

"No," replied the man.

"Do you drink a lot?"

"No."

"Do you have a vigorous sex life?"

"Yes, I do!"

"Well," said the physician, "I'm afraid with this heart murmur, you'll have to give up half your sex life."

Looking confused, the man inquired, "Which half? The looking or the thinking?"

PRENUPTIALS

A couple in their sixties were about to get married.

She said, "I want to keep my house."

He said, "That's okay with me."

She said, "And I want to keep my Mercedes."

He said, "That's fine with me too."

She said, "And I want to have sex six times a week."

He said, "That's fine with me. Put me down for Thursdays."

TOO OLD TO REMEMBER

Two clergymen were in London to attend a week's synod at Church House. They were having tea and biscuits in front of the fire, discussing how they were going to deal with the subject of the next day's conference. It was a difficult topic for clergymen—premarital sex.

"For instance," said one of them, "I never slept with my wife before I married her. Did you?"

"I can't remember," said the other. "What was her maiden name?"

ALMOST

Bernie had worked in the cookie factory all his life, never finding the time to get married. Then, one sunny morning, a beautiful eighteen-year-old girl walked on to the shop floor and it was love at first sight.

Within a month, Bernie and Kate were married and on the way to California for their honeymoon.

"So how was it?" asked Martin, Bernie's colleague, on the couple's return.

"Oh, just wonderful," replied a dewy-eyed Bernie. "The sun, the surf... and we made love almost every night. We—"

"Just a minute," interrupted Martin. "Forgive me for asking, but you made love almost every night—at your age?"

"Oh yes," said Bernie, "We almost made love Saturday, we almost made love Sunday..."

HOW LONG AGO WAS IT?

A minister decided to do something a little off the wall at his weekly sermon. He said to his parishioners, "Today, in church, I am going to say a single word. And whichever single word I say, I want you to sing whichever hymn comes to your mind. And thus we will be united in thought, in worship and in life."

The pastor shouted out "Beautiful."

Immediately, the congregation started singing, in unison, "All Things Bright and Beautiful."

The pastor hollered out "Grace."

The congregation chorused "Amazing Grace."

The pastor yelled, "Dance!"

The congregation sang "Lord of the Dance."

The pastor said, "Sex."

The congregation fell into total silence.

Everyone was in shock. They all began to look around at each other nervously, afraid to say anything.

Then, from the back of the church, in a high, reed-thin voice, a weary middle-aged woman began to sing "Precious Memories."

EVERYTHING'S PEACHY

Alex was making love to his wife when suddenly, to his immense joy, Claire let out a short cry of pleasure.

"My goodness, darling!" he exclaimed. "What happened?"

"It's amazing," replied Claire. "I finally decided that those cushions would look much better in peach."

OLD FROGS

One of the saddest things about feeling over the hill is that it can be one of the loneliest times in life. A middle-aged woman decided that she needed a pet to keep her company, so off to the pet shop she went—but nothing seemed to catch her interest, except a rather ugly frog.

As she walked by the cage he was sitting in, he seemed to look up and wink at her. She could have sworn he whispered, "I'm lonely too, buy me and you won't be sorry," but she knew her hearing was no longer good enough for whispers, so she didn't pay any attention.

As nothing else was even of vague interest, she bought the frog and walked dejectedly to her car.

As they were driving down the road, however, she heard the frog whisper again. "Kiss me, you won't be sorry," he croaked.

With nothing to lose, the woman thought, "What the heck," and gave the frog a peck on his scaly lips.

Immediately, the reptile turned into an absolutely stunning, delectable young prince. Then the prince kissed her back, and you know what the woman turned into?

The first motel she could find.

DEFINITELY OVER THE HILL!

Former U.S. senator Chauncey Depew once found himself seated at dinner next to a young woman with a very low-cut, off-the-shoulder dress. Depew, staring at the young woman's décolletage, leaned over to her and is said to have asked, "My dear, what is keeping that dress on you?"

"Only your age, Mr. Depew," replied the young woman.

AGE APPROPRIATE

A bachelor, just turned 40, began feeling desperate. "I went to a singles bar," he told a friend, "walked over to this 20-year-old woman and asked, 'Where have you been all my life?' She said, 'Teething.' "

—Mack McGinnis in *Quote*

BEAR SHOOTING

A man in his sixties was having his annual medical check-up and the doctor asked him how he was feeling.

"I've never been better!" the patient boasted. "I've got a nineteen-year-old bride who's pregnant and having my baby! What do you say to that?"

The doctor considered this for a moment, then said, "Let me tell you a story. I knew a man who was an avid hunter. He never missed a season. But one day, he went out in a bit of a hurry, and he accidentally grabbed his umbrella instead of his rifle.

"So he was in the woods, and suddenly a grizzly bear appeared right in front of him. He raised up his umbrella, pointed it at the bear and squeezed the handle. And do you know what happened?"

Dumbfounded, the man whispered, "No."

The doctor continued, "The bear dropped dead in front of him."

"That's impossible!" exclaimed the old man. "Someone else must have shot that bear."

"That's kind of what I'm getting at," replied the doctor.

UNABLE TO DRIVE?

Peter still enjoyed chasing young girls even in his fifties.

When his wife was asked if she minded, she answered, "Why should I be upset? Dogs chase cars, but they can't drive."

ALL WRAPPED UP IN ONE

Striking up a conversation with the attractive woman seated beside him on a coast-to-coast flight, a would-be Romeo asked, "What kind of man attracts you?"

"I've always been drawn to Native American men," she replied. "They're in harmony with nature."

"I see," said the man, nodding.

"But, then, I really go for Jewish men who put women on a pedestal, and I can rarely resist the way Southern gentlemen always treat their ladies with respect."

"Please allow me to introduce myself," said the man. "My name is Tecumseh Goldstein, but all my friends call me Bubba."

—Matthew W. Boyle

OPPOSITES ATTRACT

Why did you marry your husband?" asked the neighborhood gossip. "You don't seem to have much in common."

"It was the old story of opposites attracting each other," explained the wife. "I was pregnant and he wasn't."

—Parts Pups

A SECOND OPINION

A doctor and his wife were having a big argument at breakfast. "You aren't so good in bed either!" he shouted and stormed off to work. By midmorning, he decided he'd better make amends and phoned home. After many rings, his wife picked up the phone.

"What took you so long to answer?"

"I was in bed."

"What were you doing in bed this late?"

"Getting a second opinion."

—Edward B. Worby

SUPER

A 90-year-old man checked into a posh hotel to celebrate his birthday. As a surprise, some friends sent a call girl to his room. When the man answered his door, he saw before him a beautiful young woman. "I have a present for you," she said.

"Really?" replied the bewildered gent.

"I'm here to give you super sex," she said in a whisper.

"Thanks," he said thoughtfully. "I'll take the soup."

—Dorian Goldstein

Love is the answer, but while you're waiting for the answer, sex raises some pretty good questions.

—Woody Allen

ON-LINE DATING

A bachelor asked the computer to find him the perfect mate: "I want a companion who is small and cute, loves water sports, and enjoys group activities."

Back came the answer: "Marry a penguin."

—*Rainbow*

STUBBORN AS A MULE

A husband and wife drove for miles in silence after a terrible argument in which neither would budge. The husband pointed to a mule in a pasture.

"Relative of yours?" he asked.

"Yes," she replied. "By marriage."

—Bobbie Mae Cooley in *The American Legion Magazine*

SURPRISE!

Arnold complained to a coworker that he didn't know what to get his wife for her birthday. "She already has everything you could think of, and anyway, she can buy herself whatever she likes."

"Here's an idea," said the coworker. "Make up your own gift certificate that says, 'Thirty minutes of great loving, any way you want it.' I guarantee she'll be enchanted."

The next day, Arnold's coworker asked, "Well? Did you take my suggestion?"

"Yes," said Arnold.

"Did she like it?"

"Oh, yes! She jumped up, kissed me on the forehead, and ran out the door yelling, 'See you in 30 minutes!' "

—Tom Matthews

A SELF-STARTER

Kevin: "My wife and I argue a lot. She's very touchy—the least little thing sets her off."

Christopher: "You're lucky. Mine is a self-starter."

—Ron Dentinger in the
Dodgeville, Wis., *Chronicle*

A STOCK EXCHANGE

I realized that the ups and downs of the stock market had become too big a part of our life one night as my husband and I prepared for bed. As we slid beneath the covers, I snuggled up to him and told him I loved him.

Drifting off to sleep, he drowsily whispered back, "Your dividend growth fund went up three days this week."

—Shirley S. Dillon

SEX, PLEASE

People often assume that the older you get, the less likely you are to want to make love, but the following story belies all that.

A woman by the name of Millicent was living in an old people's home. One day, she walked into the occupational therapy room and proceeded to parade in front of all the other (mostly male) residents.

Then she clenched her fist and announced to the gathering: "Anyone who can guess what I have in my closed hand can have sex with me tonight."

An elderly gentleman with a twinkle in his eye replied, "A rhinoceros."

Millicent grinned. "Close enough," she said gleefully.

ASPIRIN, DEAR?

Having celebrated their thirtieth wedding anniversary with a slap-up meal at the local restaurant, Barbara thanked Billy for a lovely evening.

"Oh, but it's not finished yet," said Billy, handing her a small gold box tied with a red silk ribbon.

Barbara opened it excitedly—but there was no anniversary jewelry inside, as she had secretly hoped. Instead, two white pills nestled against the cream tissue paper.

"What are these?" asked Barbara quizzically.

"Aspirin," replied Billy.

"But I haven't got a headache."

"Gotcha!" he exclaimed with a grin.

4

The Doctor Is In

YOU KNOW YOU'RE OVER THE HILL WHEN...

- You buy a sheer, sexy negligée, but you don't know anyone whose eyesight is good enough to see through it.

- Job interviewers no longer ask you, "What do you think you'll be doing in ten years' time?"

- You have your own phone number written down somewhere, but can't remember where.

- Your favorite section of the paper is "On This Date Fifty Years Ago."

- Conversations with people your own age often turn into "duelling ailments."

- You're on a TV game show and decide to risk it all and go for the chairlift.

- You're seventeen around the neck, forty-one around the waist, and ninety-five around the golf course.

- You have too much room in the house and not enough room in the medicine cabinet.

TOOTH AND NAIL

Did you hear about the dentist who married a manicurist? They fought tooth and nail.

—Joan McCourt

GOOD NEWS AND BAD NEWS

The doctor led his patient into his office, sat her down, and said, "I have some good news and some bad news."

The woman said, "Give me the good news."

The doctor said, "They're going to name a disease after you."

SENIOR-SAFETY CAP

In 2008, a man in his mid-fifties had to be rushed to a hospital, having made his eye bleed while trying to open a bottle of pills.

He was attempting to unscrew the child-safety cap from a container of anti-inflammatory drugs, which he was taking for his arthritis, but he struggled so much that his hand flew backward and punched him hard in the face.

To add insult to injury, the nurses at the hospital then inquired if it was his wife who had hit him and offered to alert a social worker. At that point, he knew he had to give up.

"If I didn't feel old before the incident," he was quoted as saying, "I did afterward. Very, very old. Washed up, embarrassed, absolutely over the hill."

RAISING THE DEAD

A middle-aged couple were watching a healing service on a cable channel. The evangelist called to all who wanted to be healed to go to their television set, place one hand on the TV and the other hand on the body part where they needed treatment.

The wife got up and walked to the television, then placed her right hand on the set and her left hand on her arthritic shoulder that was causing her great pain. Then the husband got up, went to the TV, placed his right hand on the set and his left hand on his crotch.

His missus scowled at him and said, "I guess you just don't get it. The purpose of doing this is to heal the sick, not raise the dead."

LIVING VICARIOUSLY

"A medical report states that the human male is physically capable of enjoying sex up to and even beyond the age of eighty. Not as a participant, of course."

—Denis Norden

NO REPEATS

An anxious senior citizen telephoned her doctor. "Is it accurate to say," she demanded, "that the pills you have prescribed me must be taken till the very end of my days?"

"Yes, I'm afraid so," her GP said firmly.

There was a pause, before the lady responded, "I'm wondering, then, just how serious my condition is, because this prescription is marked 'no repeats?'"

MIRACULOUS CURES

A doctor, who was renowned for his exceptional results in treating arthritis, had a waiting room chock-full of patients.

A lady, whose back was curved into a most painful-looking arc, shuffled in slowly, bent double, relying heavily on her wooden stick. All who saw her pitied her.

When her name was called, she hobbled into the consultant's office. Incredibly, within five minutes, she emerged a new woman, walking completely upright with her head held high.

A man in the waiting room, who had seen all this, rushed up to the revived patient and declared, "My God, it's a miracle! I saw it with my own eyes. You walked in here with

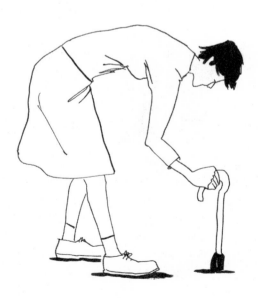

the worst arthritis I've ever seen and now you're strolling out with a totally straight back! What on earth did the doctor do?"

"He gave me a longer cane," she replied.

PLAIN TRUTH

Upon retiring, a woman decided to fulfill her lifelong dream and live abroad. As part of her preparations, she visited her doctor to pick up her medical records. The doctor asked her how she was doing, so with a sigh she reported a litany of symptoms—this aches, that's stiff, I'm not as quick as I used to be, and so on.

He responded with, "Mrs. Dickson, you have to expect things to start deteriorating. After all, who wants to live to a hundred?"

Mrs. Dickson looked him straight in the eye and replied, "Anyone who's ninety-nine."

SYMPTOMS OF GOING OVER THE HILL

"Have you not a moist eye, a dry hand, a yellow cheek, a white beard, a decreasing leg, an increasing belly? Is not your voice broken, your wind short, your chin double, your wit single, and every part about blasted with antiquity?"

—William Shakespeare, *Henry IV, Part II*

SILENCE IS GOLDEN

A couple go to church one Sunday. Halfway through the service, the wife leans over and whispers in her husband's ear, "I've just let out a silent fart. What should I do?"

The husband replies, "Put a new battery in your hearing aid."

CONFUSED?

One day at the village Post Office, the woman behind the counter watched as the local doctor, who was then in his seventies and a little forgetful, carefully tried to write out a check to cover his electricity bill.

But the doctor looked a little frustrated, not to mention puzzled.

The woman behind the counter asked the doctor what was wrong. "Perhaps I can help?" she suggested.

"Oh, I doubt it," replied the doctor, looking down at his hand, in which lay a rectal thermometer. "I was just trying to remember where I last left my pen."

IS EXERCISE BAD FOR YOU?

Exercise can be very bad for you at any age, but the older you get, the worse it can become. Australian author Clive James knows this only too well:

"Joggers are people who really believe that they can recapture their youth by taking exercise. The brutal facts suggest that unless you have never lost your youth, and have been taking exercise all the time, then trying to get fit will kill you as surely as a horse-kick to the heart."

THE DREADED MENOPAUSE

Women sometimes get to know they're over the hill when their bodies begin giving out increasingly desperate signals—otherwise known as the menopause. Here are a few ways to discover if you are experiencing "estrogen issues:"

1. Everyone around you has an attitude problem.
2. You're adding chocolate flakes to your savory pie.
3. The dryer has shrunk every last pair of your trousers.
4. Your husband is suddenly agreeing to everything you say.
5. You're using your mobile phone to dial up every bumper sticker that says: "How's my driving? Call 914 33…"

DEADLY HUMOR

A middle-aged accountant was laid up in the hospital for weeks on end. All the doctors on the ward couldn't seem to help her or diagnose what was wrong.

"Never mind," said the lady, who simply wanted to get back to her books and her numbers, "I don't need your help."

But despite her objections, the doctors still kept trying to get to the bottom of what was making her ill. Finally, when all the medics had left the ward, the lady's relatives asked her what had been decided.

"It's just like I told everyone," she said triumphantly. "I'm fine. The doctors, they used all sorts of long complicated words, which I didn't understand, but then they finally said, 'Well, there's no use worrying about it or arguing over it. The autopsy will soon give us the answer!'"

A POSITIVE SPIN

Doctor: You're going to live to be sixty.
Patient: I am sixty!
Doctor: What did I tell you?

MISPERCEPTION

"I think my wife's going deaf," Joe told their doctor.

"Try to test her hearing at home and let me know how severe her problem is before you bring her in for treatment," the doctor said.

So that evening, when his wife was preparing dinner, Joe stood 15 feet behind her and said, "What's for dinner, honey?"

No response.

He moved to ten feet behind her and asked again.

No response.

Then he stood five feet in back of her and tried again but still got no answer. Finally, he stood directly behind her and asked, "Honey, what's for supper?"

She turned around. "For the fourth time—I said chicken!"

—Gordon Bayliss

INNOVATION

Waiting for an elevator at our hospital, I stood next to a maintenance man holding a bicycle pump. Noticing my curious stare, he looked at me and remarked with a grin, "It's the new HMO oxygen program."

—Danny Galyean

PERFECT TREATMENT

When you regularly discuss with your friends and acquaintances all your various ailments, and are well informed as to which doctor is best at treating each disease, you know you're well and truly over the hill—just like the ladies in this next anecdote.

One afternoon, two women, Elsie Nash and Sybil Watts, were sitting in a pretty little café on the high street, discussing Elsie's favorite doctor.

"I don't like your GP," Sybil commented frankly, sipping her Earl Grey tea, while eyeing Elsie up and down over the rim of her cup. "He was treating old Mrs. White for chronic lung disease for over two years—and eventually she died of a heart attack."

"So?" said Elsie.

"And he was treating Robert Erskine for kidney disease for over six months and when he finally kicked the bucket, it was of liver disease."

"But what's your point?" Elsie inquired, taking a large bite out of her carrot cake.

But Sybil simply continued: "And when he was treating old Mrs. Hunt for pneumonia, she passed away from emphysema."

"I don't understand," said Elsie, now putting her cake firmly down on her plate in a gesture of frustration. "What's wrong with all of that? What are you getting at?'

"Well, when *my* doctor treats you for anything, *that's* what you die of," replied Sybil, with a triumphant smile.

SAD BUT TRUE

During my uncle's physical exam, his doctor mentioned that he was slightly overweight. "Do you get any exercise?" the physician asked.

"Well, I used to have an exercise bike in the TV room," my uncle began.

"Used to!" the doctor said. "Where is it now?"

"I had to store it in the basement," my uncle confessed, "because it got in the way of my snack trays."

—Wayne R. Reif

ROLL OVER

Patient: "This hospital is no good. They treat us like dogs."

Orderly: "Mr. Jones, you know that's not true. Now, roll over."

—Anne Wolosyn

WHO SAYS?

An 80-year-old man goes to a doctor for a checkup. The doctor is amazed at his shape. "To what do you attribute your good health?"

"I'm a turkey hunter and that's why I'm in good shape. Get up before daylight, chase turkeys up and down mountains."

The doctor says, "Well, I'm sure it helps, but there have to be genetic factors. How old was your dad when he died?"

"Who says my dad's dead?"

"You're 80 years old and your dad's alive? How old is he?"

"Dad's 100. In fact, he turkey hunted with me this morning."

"What about your dad's dad—how old was he when he died?"

"Who says my grandpa's dead?"

"You're 80 years old and your grandfather's still living? How old is he?"

"118."

"I suppose you're going to tell me he went turkey hunting this morning?"

"No. He got married."

The doctor looks at the man in amazement. "Got married? Why would a 118-year-old guy want to get married?"

The old-timer answers, "Who says he wanted to?"

—Ardell Wieczorek

IT'S TRUE

George Burns punctuated this story with a flick of his cigar. "A woman said to me, 'Is it true that you still go out with young girls?' I said yes, it's true. She said, 'Is it true that you still smoke 15 to 20 cigars a day?' I said yes, it's true. She said, 'Is it true that you still take a few drinks every day?' I said yes, it's true.

"She said, 'What does your doctor say?' I said, 'He's dead.' "

SINCERELY

The best thing about getting older is that you gain sincerity," says Tommy Smothers. "Once you learn to fake that, there's nothing you can't do."

A COURAGEOUS WOMAN

A woman and her husband interrupted their vacation to go to a dentist. "I want a tooth pulled, and I don't want Novocain because I'm in a big hurry," the woman said. "Just extract the tooth as quickly as possible, and we'll be on our way."

The dentist was quite impressed. "You're certainly a courageous woman," he said. "Which tooth is it?"

The woman turned to her husband and said, "Show him your tooth, dear."

—*Portals of Prayer*

DOUBT

A patient was anxious after a prolonged bedside discussion by hospital doctors. The head doctor even came to see him.

"Where did you get that idea?" the doctor replied.

"All the other doctors disagreed with you, didn't they?"

"To some extent, but don't worry," said the doctor consolingly. "In a similar case, I stood firm on my diagnosis—and the postmortem proved me right!"

—Abbas Ali Zahid

BED REST

A guy spots his doctor in the mall. He stops him and says, "Six weeks ago when I was in your office, you told me to go home, get into bed and stay there until you called. But you never called."

"I didn't?" the doctor says. "Then what are you doing out of bed?"

—Ron Dentinger in the Dodgeville, Wis., *Chronicle*

NO PROBLEM

A man called his doctor's office for an appointment. "I'm sorry," said the receptionist, "we can't fit you in for at least two weeks."

"But I could be dead by then!"

"No problem. If your wife lets us know, we'll cancel the appointment."

—Ron Dentinger in the Dodgeville, Wis., *Chronicle*

ONE MORE TIME

The woman went to a dentist to have her false teeth adjusted for the fifth time. She said they still didn't fit. "Well," said the dentist, "I'll do it again this time, but no more. There's no reason why these shouldn't fit your mouth easily."

"Who said anything about my mouth?" the woman answered. "They don't fit in the glass!"

—The Speaker's Handbook of Humor,
edited by Maxwell Droke

5

Triumph...
or Tragedy?

YOU KNOW YOU'RE OVER THE HILL WHEN...

- You begin carrying your senses around in your handbag: glasses, hearing aid, dentures, and so on... —Kurt Strauss

- You're interested in going home before you get to where you're going. —Alan Mainwaring

- You smile at *everyone* because you can't hear a word they're saying.

- Work is a lot less fun—and fun is a lot more work. —Joan Rivers

- Things you buy now won't wear out.

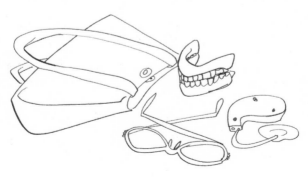

- You like telling stories... over and over and over again.

- Your children are now lying about their age.

- You can't tell the difference between a heart attack and an orgasm.

AGE-ACTIVATED ATTENTION DEFICIT DISORDER

As acronyms go, A. A. A. D. D. is one of those conditions that anyone who is over the hill must know only too well.

Browsers of the Internet (assuming, of course, that you're not already over the hill to the extent that such technological facilities are beyond your comprehension) may already be familiar with its symptoms, as countless websites list its collected traits. This is how it manifests itself.

You decide to water your garden.

As you turn on the hose in the driveway, you look over at your car and decide it needs washing.

As you start walking toward the garage for the cleaning miscellanea, you notice that there is mail on the porch table that you brought up from the mailbox earlier.

You decide to go through the mail before you wash the car.

You lay your car keys down on the table, put the junk mail in the waste basket under the table... and notice that it is full.

So you decide to put the bills back on the table and take out the trash—but then you think that since you're going to be near a mailbox when you take out the trash, you may as well pay the bills first.

You take your checkbook off the table and see that there is only one check left. Your extra checks are in your desk drawer in the study, so you go inside the house to your desk, where you find the can of Sprite that you had been drinking earlier.

You're going to look for your checks, but first you need to put the Sprite to one side, so that you don't accidentally knock it over. You notice that the Sprite is getting warm so you decide that you should put it in the refrigerator to keep it cool.

As you head toward the kitchen with the Sprite, a vase of flowers on the counter catches your eye: they need to be watered.

You place the Sprite down on the work surface—and you discover your reading glasses, for which you've been searching all morning.

You decide you better put them back on your desk in their rightful place, but first you're going to water the flowers.

You set the glasses back down on the worktop, fill a container with water—then, suddenly, you spot the TV remote. Someone has left it on the kitchen table.

You realize that tonight when you go to watch TV, you will be looking for the remote, but you know you won't remember that it's on the kitchen table, so you decide to put it back in the lounge where it belongs. First, though, you'll water the flowers.

You pour some water in the vase, but quite a bit of it spills on the floor. So you set the remote back down on the table, get some towels and wipe up the mess.

Then you head down the hall, trying to remember what you were planning to do next.

At the end of the day:

- The car isn't washed.

- The bills aren't paid.

- The trash is overflowing.

- There is a warm can of Sprite sitting on the work surface.

- The flowers don't have enough water.

- There is still only one check in your checkbook.

- You can't find the remote.

- You can't locate your glasses... and you don't remember what you did with the car keys.

Then, when you try to figure out why nothing got done today, you're really baffled, because you know you were busy all day long, and you're really tired. You realize this is a serious problem, so you make a mental note to get some help for it (which is, of course, not worth the paper it's written on). First, you see, you'll check your emails.

Afterword: you just remembered, you left the water running...

MORE HASTE, LESS SPEED

Janie was in a hurry to get to the bank before it closed. Trotting briskly to her car, she rummaged in her handbag for her keys, but couldn't find them anywhere. Realizing that her bag was already open, she figured that they must have fallen out and rolled under the car.

So, she got down on her hands and knees and crawled beneath the vehicle, contorting her body and stretching her fingers into the darkest recesses. Unable to feel the presence of the elusive keys, she decided to back out—only to discover that she was wedged fast beneath the axle.

No matter how much she tried to twist and turn, her body wouldn't move. She called out for help, but no one heard. All manner of thoughts passed through her mind: "What persuaded me to climb under the car? Why did I have that extra slice of apple pie last week?"

She lay there for two whole days until a neighbor, concerned at not having seen her, investigated a weak banging sound from under the car and found the stricken Janie. Within half an hour, firefighters had pulled her free and discovered her car keys... in the car door.

THE ATTENDANT

According to a tale related by journalist Walter Kiernan, a customer in a department store in Denmark walked into the ladies' toilets one day, only to be stared at in a very unfriendly manner by the attendant when she didn't leave a tip. The woman consequently complained to the management, who decided to do a check on the toilet attendant.

It turned out that she wasn't one of the store's employees at all, but a woman who had wandered into the restrooms a year previously and sat down to do a bit of knitting. Mistaking her for the attendant, customers began leaving her tips. So the woman had returned to the store every day, bringing her knitting with her.

MURDER MOST TIRESOME

Growing old can mean growing tedious, though the worst affected will remain convinced of their sparkling wit and bonhomie.

Foreign correspondent Frank Sparks once attended a charity function at an exclusive Park Avenue address, where he found himself unfortunately seated next to an exceedingly dull criminologist.

After listening to this man's tiresome nonsense for about half an hour, Sparks made his excuses, got up and slipped into the next room, where he bumped into the event's organizer.

"He's a bit on the boring side, isn't he?" apologized the host. Sparks nodded. "But he's got one of the finest minds in the city," the party-giver continued. "They tell me he's discovered how to commit the perfect crime."

"I know," hissed Sparks, "he almost bored me to death too."

ANOTHER WAY OF LOOKING AT IT

As my 40th birthday approached, my husband, who is a year younger, was doing his best to rub it in. Trying to figure out what all the teasing was about, our young daughter asked me, "How old is Daddy?"

"Thirty-nine," I told her.

"And how old will you be?"

"Forty," I said sadly.

"But Mommy," she exclaimed, "you're winning!"

—Kelley Martinez

NO FOOL LIKE AN OLD FOOL

A miserly old lawyer who had been diagnosed with a terminal illness was determined to prove wrong the old saying, "You can't take it with you."

After much thought and consideration, the old litigator finally devised a way of taking at least some of his money with him when he died. He told his wife to go to the bank and withdraw enough cash to fill two sacks. He then directed her to take the money to the attic and leave it directly above his bed.

His plan: when he passed away, he would reach out and grab the sacks on his way to heaven.

Several weeks after the funeral, the deceased lawyer's wife, up in the attic sorting out his things, came upon the two forgotten sacks stuffed with cash.

"Oh, that old idiot," she exclaimed. "I knew he should have had me put the money in the basement."

HELICOPTER RIDE

Charlie and his wife Deborah went to the state fair every year. They'd wander the stalls and take in the sights, and every year Charlie would say hopefully, "Deborah, I'd like to ride in that helicopter."

But Debbie always talked him down. "I know, Charlie," she'd say, "but that helicopter ride is fifty dollars—and fifty dollars is fifty dollars."

One year, as usual, they went to the fair, but Charlie was determined that this trip would be different. He said firmly to his wife, "Deborah, I'm sixty-five years old. If I don't ride that helicopter now, I might never get another chance."

Deborah pointed out, "Charlie, that helicopter ride is fifty dollars—and fifty dollars is fifty dollars."

The pilot happened to overhear the couple's quarrel and stepped in to play the peacemaker—but with a mischievous glint in his eye. He said, "Folks, I'll make you a deal. I'll take the both of you for a ride. If you can stay quiet for the entire ride and not say a word, I won't charge you. But if you say one word, it's fifty dollars."

Charlie and Deborah agreed and the flight began. The pilot took the opportunity to perform all kinds of fancy maneuvers, but he didn't hear a peep from his passengers, not even when they looped the loop. He executed his daredevil tricks over and over again, but still not a word.

When they landed, the pilot turned round to Charlie and exclaimed, "That's amazing. I did everything I possibly could to make you yell out, but you didn't—not once. I'm impressed!"

Charlie responded, "Well, to be quite honest, I almost said something when Debbie fell out, but you know—fifty dollars is fifty dollars."

GLAD TIDINGS

A sixty-year-old woman was walking along when she heard a voice from above: "You will live to be a hundred." She looked around and didn't see anyone. Again, she heard: "You will live to be a hundred."

"Oh," she thought to herself, "that was the voice of God. I've got forty more years to live!"

So off she went to the plastic surgeon. She got her whole body fixed up—face lift, boob job, bottom lift, liposuction, Botox, collagen, nose. You name it, it was now transformed.

As soon as she left the surgeon's office, she got hit by a car, passed away, and finally ascended to heaven.

She said to God accusingly, "You told me I would live to be a hundred. I was supposed to have had forty more years. So how come you let the car kill me?"

God said, "I didn't recognize you."

A NEW WRINKLE

I was hospitalized with an awful sinus infection that caused the entire left side of my face to swell. On the third day, the nurse led me to believe that I was finally recovering when she announced excitedly, "Look, your wrinkles are coming back!"

—Frances M. Krueger

CHOP, CHOP

The stereotypical middle-aged spinster with a fondness for felines was sitting in front of the fire with her favorite tomcat on her knee. Suddenly, there was a loud bang, a puff of smoke, and a twinkling fairy appeared out of the fire.

"I can grant you three wishes," the fairy announced. "What would you like?"

When she had recovered from the shock, the pragmatic woman answered, "Given the credit crunch, first I would like to be financially secure and live in comfortable surroundings till the end of my days."

With a flick of her wand, the fairy turned the room into a splendid parlor and produced many sacks of gold.

"Next wish, please," she said.

"Please make me young and beautiful," pleaded the downtrodden senior, and she was immediately transformed into a beautiful brunette. "For my third wish, will you please turn my tomcat into a handsome young man?"

Instantly, standing before her was a fine specimen of manhood, who stepped forward and took the lady's hand and kissed it, saying, "Aren't you sorry now that you took me to the vet?"

BENEFITS

A retired gentleman went to apply for Social Security. After waiting in line for what seemed an eternity, he was finally able to present himself at the relevant desk. The woman behind the counter asked him for his passport to verify his age. The man searched his pockets and realized with a sinking heart that he had left his wallet and all his ID at home.

"Will I have to go home and come back now?" he asked, giving a slightly pathetic sigh.

The woman paused and then said, "Unbutton your shirt."

The man opened his shirt, revealing lots of grey chest hair.

The woman said, "That silver hair is proof enough for me," and she processed his application.

When he got back home, the man told his wife all about his experience at the Social Security office. She responded, "You should have dropped your pants—you might have qualified for disability, too."

NAUGHTY OLD MAN

A long-suffering wife came home one lunchtime and found her husband of many years amorously involved with a young floozy in the bedroom. The woman was understandably outraged, especially as she had not had a whisper of physical affection from her spouse in a very, very long time. She had in all honesty thought him impotent.

During the quarrel that resulted, she pushed her husband off the balcony of their seventeenth-floor apartment. She was charged with murder and tried.

"But Your Honor," she said, "I didn't mean to hurt him."

"You didn't mean to hurt him?" the judge asked. "Ma'am, you pushed him off the balcony from the seventeenth floor."

"Yes," she said, "but all those things I had just seen him doing, I thought if he could do them, surely he could fly!"

EIGHTY NOT OUT!

On reaching his eightieth birthday, the actor and raconteur Sir Peter Ustinov quipped, "I feel I can talk with more authority now, especially when I say, 'I don't know.'"

SENIOR'S SPEECH

The end of your youth is nigh once you go on and on and on in an increasingly nonsensical manner, much like Sir Laurence Olivier did when he was presented with a special Oscar at the Academy Awards in 1979.

"Mr. President and governors of the Academy," he began, "committee members, fellows, my very noble and approved good masters, my friends, my fellow students in the great wealth, the great firmament of your nation's generosities, this particular choice may perhaps be found by future generations as a trifle eccentric, but the mere fact of it, the prodigal, pure, human kindness of it, must be seen as a beautiful star in that firmament which shines upon me at this moment, dazzling me a little, but filling me with warmth and the extraordinary elation, the euphoria that happens to so many of us at the first breath of the majestic glow of the new tomorrow.

"From the top of this moment, in the solace, in the kindly emotion that is charging my soul and my heart at this moment, I thank you for this great gift which lends me such a very splendid part in this glorious occasion. Thank you."

WHY WON'T YOU BELIEVE ME?

No one believes seniors... everyone thinks they are senile.

One day, a couple were celebrating their fiftieth anniversary. They had married as childhood sweethearts and had moved back to their old neighborhood after they'd retired. Holding hands, they walked back to their old school. The building was locked, but they strolled around the grounds and found the tree trunk on which Trevor had carved "I love you, Penny."

On their way back home, a bag of money fell out of an armored car, practically landing at their feet. Penny quickly picked it up. Not sure what to do with it, they took it home with them. There, Penny counted the money—all seventy thousand dollars of it.

Trevor said instantly, "We've got to give it back."

But Penny responded, "Finders keepers."

She put the money back in the bag and hid it in their attic.

The next day, two policemen were canvassing the neighborhood, looking for the money. They knocked on the door. "Pardon me, but did either of you find a bag that fell out of an armored car yesterday?' they inquired.

Penny said, "No."

Trevor said, "She's lying. She hid it up in the attic."

Penny said, "Don't believe him, he's getting senile."

The cops turned to Trevor and started to question him.

One said: "Tell us the story from the beginning."

So Trevor gave a little cough, and began: "Well, when Penny and I were walking home from school yesterday..."

The first policeman turned to his partner and said, "We're outta here."

A DIEHARD FAN

Surprised to see an empty seat at the Super Bowl, a diehard fan remarked about it to a woman sitting nearby.

"It was my husband's," the woman explained, "but he died."

"I'm very sorry," said the man. "Yet I'm really surprised that another relative, or friend, didn't jump at the chance to take the seat reserved for him."

"Beats me," she said. "They all insisted on going to the funeral."

—Coffee Break

QUITE A RECEPTION

An attorney died and went to heaven. As he approached the Pearly Gates, he noticed an orchestra playing and thousands of angels cheering. St. Peter himself rushed over to shake the lawyer's hand. "This is quite a reception," marveled the new arrival.

"You're very special," St. Peter explained. "We've never had anyone live to be 130 before."

The attorney was puzzled. "But I'm only 65."

St. Peter thought for a moment. "Oh," he said, "we must have added up your billing hours."

—David Micus

BRIGHT LIGHTS

They say when you die you see bright light at the end of a tunnel," notes comedian Ed Marques. "I think my father will see the light, then flip it off to save electricity."

—*Comic Strip Live*, Fox TV

ON PAPER

I sat there waiting for my new doctor to make his way through the file that contained my very extensive medical history. After he finished all 17 pages, he looked up at me.

"You look better in person than you do on paper."

—Carolyn Blankenship

RAIN OR SHINE

Getting hold of the wrong end of the stick is an affliction that increases with age. Worse still is the blasé way in which we nonchalantly reveal our senior selves. Thoughtless statements, thick with miscomprehension, fall as raindrops from our lips—giving all around a good soaking.

One Sunday, for example, a minister was preaching his sermon about the Lord's wisdom in caring for his flock by treating them much like a gardener might treat his plants.

"For instance," he said, "our Lord knows which of us fares best in full sunlight and which of us prospers best in the shade. Among us there are roses and heliotrope and geraniums, which flourish in the sunshine. But some of us are more like hellebores, which must be kept in a shady nook."

After he had finished, a middle-aged woman came up to him, seemingly rejuvenated by what he had taught in church.

"Oh my goodness!" she exclaimed, taking the minister's hand and squeezing it appreciatively. "That was fantastic. I am so pleased I attended this service."

The pastor's heart glowed with pride—at long last he had reached out and truly touched another's soul.

"Yes," the woman continued, "I am so pleased I came this morning. I never knew before what was wrong with my hellebores."

THE EXCEPTION TO THE RULE

The following is from a seventy-eight-year-old English woman who definitely *wasn't* past her prime when she wrote this letter to her bank manager (who was so impressed that he forwarded it to *The Times*). It gives us all hope that when we grow old, our faculties too might just remain intact.

Dear Sir,

I am writing to thank you for bouncing my check, with which I endeavored to pay my plumber last month.

By my calculations, three "nanoseconds" must have elapsed between his presenting the check and the arrival in my account of the funds needed to honor it. I refer, of course, to the automatic monthly deposit of my pension, an arrangement which, I admit, has been in place for only eight years.

You are to be commended for seizing that brief window of opportunity, and also for debiting my account $30 by way of penalty for the inconvenience caused to your bank.

My thankfulness springs from the manner in which this incident has caused me to rethink my errant financial ways.

I noticed that whereas I personally attend to your telephone calls and letters, when I try to contact you, I am confronted by the impersonal, overcharging, pre-recorded, faceless entity which your bank has become.

From now on, I, like you, choose only to deal with a flesh-and-blood person.

My mortgage and loan payments will therefore and hereafter no longer be automatic, but will arrive at your bank by check, addressed personally and confidentially to an employee at your bank whom you must nominate.

Be aware that it is an offense under the Postal Act for any other person to open such an envelope.

Please find attached an Application Contact Status, which I require your chosen employee to complete.

I am sorry it runs to eight pages, but in order that I know as much about him or her as your bank knows about me, there is no alternative. Please note that all copies of his or her medical history must be countersigned by a solicitor, and the mandatory details of his/her financial situation (income, debts, assets and liabilities) must be accompanied by documented proof.

In due course, I will issue your employee with a PIN number which he/she must quote in dealings with me. I regret that it cannot be shorter than twenty-eight digits, but, again, I have modeled it on the number of button presses required of me to access my account balance on your phone bank service.

As they say, imitation is the sincerest form of flattery.

Let me level the playing field even further. When you call me, press buttons as follows:

1. To make an appointment to see me.

2. To query a missing payment.

3. To transfer the call to my living room in case I am there.

4. To transfer the call to my bedroom in case I am sleeping.

5. To transfer the call to my toilet in case I am attending to nature.

6. To transfer the call to my mobile phone if I am not at home.

7. To leave a message on my computer. (A password to access my computer is re-quired. A password will be communicated to you at a later date to the Authorized Contact.)

8. To return to the main menu and listen to options 1 through 8.

9. To make a general complaint or inquiry, the contact will then be put on hold, pending the attention of my automated answering service. While this may, on occasion, involve a lengthy wait, uplifting music will play for the duration of the call.

Regrettably, but again following your example, I must also levy an establishment fee to cover the setting up of this new arrangement.

May I wish you a happy, if ever so slightly less prosperous, New Year.

—Your Humble Client

TALKS TO HIMSELF

Our economics professor talks to himself. Does yours?"
"Yes, but he doesn't realize it. He thinks we're listening!"

—Charisma B. Ramos

YOUR CHIPS ARE UP

A man lay frail and gasping on his deathbed. Each breath taken was a valiant struggle to survive. With his last, painful inhalation, however, he suddenly smelled the scent of his favorite chocolate-chip cookies drifting up from the kitchen below... and felt somewhat rejuvenated. He gathered his remaining strength and staggered from his bed.

Leaning heavily against the wall, he gradually made his way from the bedroom and, step by slow step, crawled downstairs on his hands and knees.

The kitchen was now mere feet away. The sunlit room beckoned with its fragrant charm. Were it not for the hacking cough that wrought his body every few paces, he would have thought himself already passed on and in nirvana. For there, spread out upon wire trays on the kitchen surfaces, were literally hundreds of his favorite chocolate-chip cookies.

Was it heaven? Or was it one final act of heroic love from his devoted wife, seeing to it that he left this world a happy man?

Mustering one great final effort, he crawled toward the table and arranged his withered limbs to sit piously at its foot. His parched lips parted; he could almost taste that familiar cookie dough, seemingly bringing him back to life.

He couldn't stop his wrinkled hand from shaking as it stretched out toward a cookie at the very edge of the table, just within reach. Suddenly, his hand was smacked, hard, with a spatula wielded by his wife.

"Stay out of those," she said. "They're for the funeral."

OBSERVE CAREFULLY

During a lecture for medical students, the professor listed as the two best qualities of a doctor the ability to conquer revulsion and the need for keen powers of observation. He illustrated this by stirring a messy substance with his finger and then licking his finger clean. Then he called a student to the front and made him do the same.

Afterward the professor remarked, "You conquered your revulsion, but your powers of observation are not very good. I stirred with my forefinger, but I licked my middle finger."

—S.K.D.

6

Thanks for the Memory

YOU KNOW YOU'RE OVER THE HILL WHEN...

- You've got more bottles in your medicine cabinet than you have in your wine cellar.

- You run out of breath walking *down* a flight of stairs.

- You choose your films by how comfy the seats are in each cinema.

- Even your birthday suit needs pressing.   —Bob Hope

- You can still fill your own car up with oil, but you can't remember how to open the bonnet.

- You look both ways before crossing a room.

- You stoop to tie your shoelaces and wonder what else you could do while you're down there.   —George Burns

- Your idea of exercise is bending over to pick up your wig.

- You arrive home from the airport by taxi to discover your car has been stolen, only for the police to phone to tell you they've found it right where you parked it back at the airport.

FANCY-FREE

"They tell you that you'll lose your mind when you grow older. What they don't tell you is that you won't miss it very much."

—Malcolm Cowley

FORGET SOMETHING?

Often the first sign of aging is when you start forgetting things, but a certain shoplifter took this to extremes one day when trying to make a quick getaway from a Dutch supermarket.

The forty-five-year-old thief, who stole a large packet of meat from a shop in the southern town of Kerkade, had run swiftly to his car, even pushing out of his way a supermarket employee who had tried to stop him by throwing himself across the car's hood.

However, the light-fingered gentleman had made one serious error: he'd forgotten his twelve-year-old son back in the supermarket. Police later arrested the man—having reunited him with the boy.

BIG MISTAKE

Forgetting your passport when you're going on holiday is not a good idea, nor is leaving your bag on a bus, but one violinist took forgetfulness to real extremes recently when he left $270,000 worth of seventeenth-century Italian violin on a train luggage rack.

"I thought I couldn't possibly forget it,' he said. 'It was just one of those terrible moments when I realized, as the train was steaming off, that I had."

DÉJÀ VU?

Renowned for his absent-mindedness, the former publisher of the *New York Post*, J. David Stern, was once hurrying down the street when he bumped into an old friend, who invited him for lunch.

Stern agreed, although he asked if they could go to a nearby restaurant as he was already running late.

They entered the establishment and sat down at a table, but when it came to making an order, Stern couldn't understand why he didn't feel very hungry.

"I beg your pardon, sir," said the waiter, "but you just finished lunch five minutes ago."

I'M OUT

According to Owen Chadwick in his biography of Michael Ramsey, who was later to become Archbishop of Canterbury, one day Ramsey left his lodgings in Boston, Lincolnshire without his front door key.

After taking a short walk, he went back and rang his doorbell to gain entrance, but his landlady was so nervous of strangers that she called out to him through the letter box that she couldn't open the door because "Mr. Ramsey is out."

"Never mind," replied the absent-minded Ramsey. "I'll return later."

HEADLESS CHICKEN

When you start forgetting your lines, like actor Paul Bailey apparently did when he appeared at Britain's Stratford-upon-Avon in *Richard III*, you know you're getting on in life.

In the production, Christopher Plummer was playing the title role while Bailey took the part of Lovell, who during Act III has to appear on stage and say the line, "Here is the head of that ignoble traitor, the dangerous and unsuspected Hastings."

However, on the night in question, Bailey completely forgot his line and instead simply stared at Plummer for what seemed like ages.

Eventually, Plummer had to help him out by asking, "Is that the head of that ignoble traitor, the dangerous and unsuspected Hastings?"

To which Bailey simply replied, "Yes."

A. E. MATTHEWS

For an actor, who has to learn hundreds of lines, growing old is particularly difficult and nowhere is this better illustrated than in the case of A. E. Matthews, who is once said to have reassured the director of the play he was working on: "I know you think I'm not going to learn my lines, but I promise you that even if we had to open next Monday, I would be all right."

"But Matty," replied the director, "we *do* open next Monday!"

A COUPLE OF OLD JOKES

In the excellent *2,500 Anecdotes for All Occasions,* edited by Edmund Fuller, there are many jokes about being over the hill, but the following two about forgetful professors are definitely my favorites.

1. "That absent-minded Professor Schmaltz has left his umbrella again. He'd leave his head if it were loose," observed the waiter.

   "That's true," said the manager. "I just heard him say he was going to Switzerland for his lungs."

2. "Did you see this?" the professor's wife asked him as he arrived home. "There's a report in the paper of your death."

   "Dear me," replied her husband. "We must remember to send a wreath."

BOILING POINT

Even distinguished scientists like Sir Isaac Newton can suffer lapses of memory, as the following story attests.

One day, a kitchen maid in Sir Isaac's house found the great man standing in front of a large pot of boiling water. He looked down at his hand, in which he was holding an egg, then glanced at the pot: at the bottom lay his watch.

WHAT DID I JUST SAY?

As we all know, life can be a matter of the blind leading the blind, as this letter to *Reader's Digest* clearly demonstrates. Even our teachers are subject to being over the hill, it seems. Michelle Salter wrote in November 2007:

> During an intensive training course, I said to the instructor, "I don't know how I'll remember all this information for the test."
>
> "I've been using mind-mapping techniques for twenty years to help me memorize things," he told me. "Actually, I've run courses on the subject."
>
> The chat drifted on to other matters, but, intrigued by his mention of his techniques, I approached the instructor over lunch.
>
> "Do you still do mind-mapping instruction?"
>
> "Yes, I do," he said, looking surprised. "How did you know about that?"

SOME VERY WISE WORDS

Curly-haired, angelic-looking Harpo Marx, whose other trademarks included playing the harp and never speaking on film, was one of the famous Marx brothers (alongside Chico and Groucho). Loved by millions all over the world for the films he and his brothers made, off screen he was no less humorous—particularly when it came to making fun of old age.

"Many years ago," he wrote in his autobiography, "a very wise man named Bernard Baruch took me aside and put his arm around my shoulder.

"'Harpo, my boy,' he said, 'I'm going to give you three pieces of advice, three things you should always remember.'

"My heart jumped and I glowed with expectation. I was going to hear the magic password to a rich, full life from the master himself.

"'Yes, sir?' I said. And he told me the three things.

"I regret I've forgotten what they were."

WHO'S OVER THE HILL?

Chefs are not renowned for their forgetfulness, but one short-order cook was obviously feeling over the hill on the day a couple of teenagers walked into his restaurant and ordered two hamburgers.

All morning long, the chef, Simon Martin, had been shouting at the restaurant's waitresses because they kept forgetting to take his orders to the tables. He prided himself

on serving up meals as speedily as possible, so he was concerned that their sluggishness reflected badly on him.

Yet pride, it seems, comes before a fall. After the two young men had placed their order, Martin quickly executed the dishes and rang the bell to alert the waiting staff that the food was ready. Imagine how happy the waitresses were when, having promptly served up the meals to the two boys, the pair complained that the chef had forgotten to put the burgers inside the buns!

A RIGHT ROYAL TO-DO

Most men can remember a pretty girl's face quite easily, so British prime minister Benjamin Disraeli must really have been over the hill when the following occurred.

One day, while talking to a friend, he remarked that he could not recall a particular inn that had been mentioned.

The friend protested: "You must remember the place, sir. There was a very handsome barmaid there—monstrous fine gal. You must have been in the King's Arms, sir."

"Perhaps," responded Disraeli, "if I had been in *her* arms, I might have remembered it."

IT'S BEEN 10 YEARS

A man walked into a crowded New York City restaurant and caught the eye of a harried waiter. "You know," he said, "it's been 10 years since I came in here."

"Don't blame me," the waiter snapped. "I'm working as fast as I can."

—Norton Mockridge, United Features Syndicate

LOST FOR WORDS

You know you're over the hill when your mind goes completely blank—but never is this more inopportune than when people are waiting to hear what you have to say, as happened to politician John G. Winant.

Once, when asked to make a speech in England, Winant stood in agonized silence for four minutes, before finally whispering: "The worst mistake I ever made was in getting up in the first place."

7

Life's
Little Slips

YOU KNOW YOU'RE OVER THE HILL WHEN...

- The creaking in your house is coming from your knees.

- There's nothing left to learn the hard way.

- Your TV is as loud as it can get and you still can't hear it.

- You no longer reach for the moon. In fact, you have difficulty reaching for your toes.

- You find yourself beginning to like accordion music.

- You realize time's a great healer, but it's a lousy beautician.

- Your little black book only contains names ending in M.D.

- Your broad mind and your narrow waist begin to change places.
  —E. Cossman

IN A MUDDLE

British TV broadcaster Hugh Scully must know all about feeling over the hill, for at the end of a BBC television interview with Liza Minelli on the program *Nationwide*, he apparently ended the Q-and-A session by saying, "Thank you, Judy Garland."

Luckily, Minelli was in good form that day and saved the moment by replying, "I'll tell Liza."

WHICH WAY ARE YOU GOING?

Some people know they're past their prime when they forget where they've put their car keys, others when they forget where they've parked the car, but one woman caused mayhem in March 2008 when she drove for fifteen miles up the wrong side of a major highway!

According to an article in *The Times*, the woman became confused when confronted with a "new traffic configuration" at a roundabout. Police followed the car for seven exits until they could bring her to a halt.

In mitigation, she explained, "There was nowhere to turn around."

WHAT A DOPE

A forty-five-year-old Chinese farmer accidentally knocked himself out for eleven hours while he was supposed to be anesthetizing deer. After administering a tranquilizing shot to a deer, Mr. Liu noticed anesthetic dripping from the needle and, while using his hand to wipe it, somehow contrived to inject himself.

EASY ON THE TEETH

"At the harvest festival in our church, the area behind the pulpit was piled high with tins of fruit for the old-age pensioners. We had collected the tinned fruit from door to door. Most of it came from old-age pensioners."

—Clive James

WHO IS THAT MAN?

For many years, Groucho Marx and the bestselling author Sidney Sheldon were close Hollywood friends and neighbors. In his eighties, Groucho was in the habit of popping round to visit Sheldon and his wife every afternoon for a little snack of an apple and a chunk of cheese.

"It became such a ritual," Sheldon recalled, "that my wife and I looked forward to it every day."

However, when the Sheldons decided to rent out their Hollywood mansion and move to Rome, confusion ensued.

One morning, Sidney received a letter from his tenant saying: "We love the house, but there is one strange thing. Every afternoon, there is a little old man, between eighty-five and ninety, who knocks at our door and asks for some cheese and an apple. Can you tell us who he is?"

SIR JOHN GIELGUD

One evening, the inimitable actor Sir John Gielgud was in his dressing room, having just come off stage, when a man entered the room to congratulate him on his performance.

"How pleased I am to meet you," exclaimed Sir John, who recognized the man's face. "I used to know your son, we were at school together."

"I don't have a son," replied the man somewhat crossly. "*I* was the one who was at school with you."

INDECENT PROPOSAL

Three magistrates were trying a case of indecent assault. It was a sweltering morning and the courtroom was very hot.

On the chairwoman's right was a conscientious schoolteacher, while on her left was a retired admiral with a very gray beard. As frequently happens when you're getting on in life, he began to nod off and was soon fast asleep as the chairwoman asked the young woman in the witness box to write down what the accused man had said to her.

The girl wrote something down on a slip of paper, which was handed up to the chairwoman, who read it and then nudged the sleeping admiral to wake him. He gave a snort and woke up to find the following note being passed to him: "I'm feeling really horny. What about coming back to my place for a quick one?"

He read it with horror and hastily handed it back to the chairwoman, whispering, "Madam, control yourself. You must be out of your mind!"

TIMBER!

In 2001, a tree surgeon suffered a major—and costly—senior moment on the job.

His client had asked him to cut down a beech tree, the roots of which were damaging the foundations of his house. However, the tree surgeon felled the wrong tree —an irreplaceable ninety-year-old oak!

He was later made to pay his customer a substantial sum in damages after a court decided he was in breach of contract. Being over the hill was simply no defense.

FOOT-IN-MOUTH DISEASE

Often, knowing you're over the hill coincides with the time you open your mouth and say completely the wrong thing.

One day, an elderly woman was visiting a long-lost relative's house for tea. Her hostess's young son ran up to her as she entered the house and blurted out, "My, how ugly you are."

Horrified, the child's mother remonstrated, "Zack! What do you mean, calling Mrs. Winters ugly?"

"I only meant it as a joke," replied the little boy.

"Well," said the mother, clearly without thinking through her reply, "how much better would the joke have been if you had said to our guest, 'My, how pretty you are!'"

MIXED UP?

After giving his Sunday sermon, a bishop was standing by the cathedral doors, thanking his congregation as they made their way out, when an enthused lady walked up to him.

"Bishop," she gushed, "you'll never know what your service meant to me. It was just like water to a drowning man!"

FOILED BY A CHECK

Bank robbers really don't have a lot to remember when they go out on a job, so Kevin Thompson must have thought he was completely over the hill when, in 1987, he went to rob the Mid-Atlantic National Bank in Bloomfield, New Jersey, but forgot to take his hold-up note with him.

Consequently, he decided to improvise and scrawled his note on the back of one of his checks, which he then handed to a teller.

After the robbery had taken place, the teller duly handed in the note to the police. With all the relevant information it provided for them, the cops promptly went straight to Mr. Thompson's address and arrested him.

FINISHED YET?

Going on and on and on is often a good indication that you are over the hill. After all, part of the art of giving a good speech is knowing exactly when to stop—hence the inclusion of the following joke.

"Has he finished yet?" asked a victim of a particularly long oration being given by an elderly professor at Oxford.

"Yes," came his companion's reply. "He finished a long time ago, but he just won't stop."

DO YOU KNOW WHO YOU ARE?

Among all the excellent collections of quotes, quips and anecdotes that Jacob Braude included in his *Toastmaster's Handbook*, the following story is the perfect example of someone receiving due warning that he was definitely on his way to getting old.

"The man in the barber's chair was comfortably emulsified under a pack of steaming towels, when suddenly a boy rushed into the shop, shouting, 'Mr. Balsam, Mr. Balsam, your store is on fire!'

"Horrified, the customer leaped from his chair, ripped off the apron and sped wildly up the street. After two or three blocks, he stopped suddenly, scratched his head and cried out in great perplexity: 'What in the heck am I doing? My name isn't Balsam.'"—Norton Mockridge, United Features

ROUGH DAY

"It's been a rough day. I got up this morning, put on a shirt and a button fell off. I picked up my briefcase and the handle came off. I'm afraid to go to the bathroom."

—Rodney Dangerfield

LADIES AND GENTLEMEN

Not knowing where you are is usually the preserve of explorers who have lost their compass and maps, but occasionally, it is an early indication that you are over the hill, as the following anecdote testifies.

A woman entered a room in a London hotel, where she immediately recognized a well-known British politician pacing up and down, up and down. The woman asked the gentleman what he was doing there.

"I'm about to give an after-dinner speech," he said.

"And do you always get so nervous before you are called upon to deliver them?" she asked, not unreasonably.

"Nervous?" he replied. "I'm not nervous. In fact, I never get nervous."

"Then what are you doing," demanded the woman, "in the ladies' room?"

MARITAL IGNORANCE IS BLISS

An Australian hoping to move to Hawaii with his Hawaiian wife in 2008 forgot that he had married someone else thirty years earlier. U.S. immigration officials ruled his latest marriage invalid, but despite being shown his signature on the 1978 license, the man had no recollection of the ceremony. He did, however, vaguely remember a "nice" blonde from Arizona around that time...

KEEP DEATH OFF THE ROADS

After reserving her seventy-five-year-old grandfather a seat on a flight from New York to Florida, Jane called the airline to go over his special needs. The representative listened patiently as Jane requested a wheelchair and an attendant for her granddad because of his arthritis and impaired vision to the point of near blindness.

Jane's apprehension lightened a bit when the assistant promised her that everything would be taken care of, so she sincerely expressed her gratitude for the good service.

"Oh, you're welcome," the representative replied.

Jane was about to hang up when the woman cheerfully asked, "And will your grandfather need a rental car?"

PICTURE IMPERFECT

A picture researcher of a certain age received a particularly difficult request from a client, but was keen to reply in a positive manner and prove that she was willing to go the extra mile.

However, while drafting her response, she accidentally leaned on her keyboard and ended up typing !!$%%&**!££!*%$**&!£%*! She was so flustered at having written what read like an expletive that in her haste to delete the message, she compounded the error by sending it.

AN HONEST DAY'S WORK

Some people aren't cut out for a life of crime, as is aptly demonstrated by the following news story about a thief who stormed into a Kwik Shop in Topeka, Kansas.

On finding that there wasn't enough cash in the register, he tied up the shop assistant... and then worked the register himself for three hours, before police turned up and arrested him.

HARD OF HEARING

A couple are driving cross-country and the woman is at the wheel. She gets pulled over by the highway patrol.

The officer walks over to her car and says, "Ma'am, did you know you were speeding?"

The woman turns to her husband and asks, "What did he say?"

The man yells, "HE SAYS YOU WERE SPEEDING."

The patrolman says, "May I see your license, please?"

The woman turns to her husband and asks, "What did he say?"

The man yells, "HE WANTS TO SEE YOUR DRIVER'S LICENSE."

The woman gives him her license.

The patrolman says, "I see you are from Texas. I spent some time there once. Had the worst sex with a woman I have ever had."

The woman turns to her husband and asks, "What did he say?"

The man yells, "HE THINKS HE KNOWS YOU."

UNDERLAY

In 2008, in an attempt to save money, Nicola Williams of Port Isaac, Cornwall, decided to lay a new carpet in her bedroom herself.

She pulled up the old carpet before smoothly laying down the replacement—but, unable to locate her glasses at the crucial moment, didn't notice that she'd buried her dog's favorite squeaky toy beneath the new rug. (Her myopic eyes didn't see the strange bulge under the floor.)

Two days and much barking later, the toy was finally retrieved.

AND FOR THE DEFENSE

Charged with armed robbery of a grocery store, a forty-seven-year-old man by the name of Dennis Newton decided to dismiss his lawyers and mount his own defense. Assistant district attorney Larry Jones said that Newton was doing quite a fair job of representing himself until the store manager testified that Newton was the robber.

Suddenly, Newton completely lost it and shouted: "I should have blown your f*****g head off!" before quickly realizing his mistake and adding, "If I'd been the one that was there."

The jury subsequently took only a few minutes to convict Newton, who was then handed a thirty-year jail sentence.

MISREADINGS

You know you're over the hill when you can't read words properly... as the following joke illustrates beautifully.

Two older Jewish women, Rebecca and Anne, are at their painting class one morning, when Rebecca says to Anne, "Wish me good luck. My son finally met a girl and maybe they will get married. But the only thing my son said is that she has herpes. What is herpes?"

Anne replied, "I don't know, but I have a medical encyclopedia at home and I will research it for you."

The next day the ladies meet again, this time at Pilates, and Anne says to her friend, "'Becca, it's OK. You don't have to worry. It's a disease of the gentiles."

TONGUE-TWISTERS

You know you're over the hill when you start getting all your metters lixed up and begin using incorrect words... much like Mrs. Levi Zeiglerheiter did, according to Kenneth Rose in his book *Superior Person*, published in 1969. Apparently, upon arriving in New York after a stormy ocean crossing, Mrs. Zeiglerheiter exclaimed, "At last I am back on terracotta."

Similarly, according to Nigel Rees in his excellent *Cassell's Dictionary of Anecdotes*, a certain law student, when asked what was necessary for a marriage to be rendered lawful in Scotland, replied: "For a marriage to be valid in Scotland, it is absolutely necessary that it should be consummated in the presence of two policemen."

Then there's the story about the dear old grandmother who, on hearing the Beatles' song "Lucy in the Sky with Diamonds," thought they had sung that the girl with "kaleidoscope eyes" was actually the girl with "colitis goes by!" Medical ailments were clearly on her mind.

Finally, there is the story, first told by Kenneth Williams in *The Kenneth Williams Diaries* (1993), about his aged mother, who announced one day, "Oh! They're opening a lesbian restaurant there!"

Kenneth corrected her: "It's Lebanese," but his mother then went on: "Yes. They're all over the place now, aren't they?"

RECORD HOLDER

Back at my high school for the tenth reunion, I met my old coach. Walking through the gym, we came upon a plaque on which I was still listed as the record holder for the longest softball throw.

Noticing my surprise, the coach said, "That record will stand forever."

I was about to make some modest disclaimer that records exist to be broken, when he added, "We stopped holding that event years ago."

—Gene Head

CHOICES

My hearing had gotten worse, and ultimately I was faced with a decision: buy a pontoon boat, which I could enjoy all summer, or get a hearing aid. The choice was obvious—to me at least. However, my sisters did not approve of the boat.

One day during lunch with them, I was having trouble following the conversation. Finally I leaned over to one of my sisters and asked what had just been said.

"You should have brought along your pontoon boat," she replied.

—Betty Jo Hendrick

OUCH!

Turning 50 two years ago, I took a lot of good-natured ribbing from family and friends. So as my wife's 50th birthday approached, I decided to get in some needling of my own. I sat her down, looked deep into her eyes, then said I had never made love to anyone who was over 50 years old.

"Oh, well, I have," she deadpanned. "It's not that great."

—Bob Moreland

8

Shall We Celebrate?

YOU KNOW YOU'RE OVER THE HILL WHEN...

- You receive two invitations to go out on the same night, and choose to attend the event that gets you home the earliest.

- You sit in a rocking chair and can't get it started.

- You confuse having a clear conscience with having a bad memory.

- You wonder how you could be over the hill when you don't ever remember reaching the top of it.

- You are cautioned to slow down by the doctor instead of the police.

- Traveling isn't as much fun because all the ancient sites are younger than you are.

- Every time you suck in your gut, your ankles swell.

- Your investment in health insurance is finally beginning to pay off.

- Your secrets are safe with your friends—because they can't remember them either.

TOO OLD TO CARE

On being sent an invitation by a leading society hostess to the effect that she would be "at home" that day, a curmudgeonly George Bernard Shaw is said to have replied, "So will G. Bernard Shaw."

TAKING THE BLAME

A farmer and his wife were standing outside their chicken coop, watching the chicks feed on grain, when the woman happily recalled that the next month would mark their silver wedding anniversary.

"Let's throw a party, Dave," she suggested. "Let's kill a chicken."

The farmer scratched his grizzled head. "Gee, Annie," he finally answered, "I don't see why the chicken should take the blame for something that happened twenty-five years back."

TYPO?

Lawrence Dunham, who really hoped he *wasn't* over the hill, wrote this letter to *Reader's Digest*.

"To celebrate my retirement, my wife and I dined with a friend we hadn't seen for years. The next day, he sent us an email that included, I hope, a typo: 'How wonderful it was to see you both aging.'"

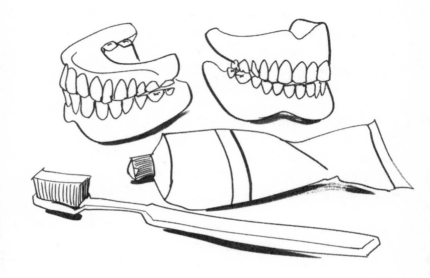

SWAPSIES

A rather mature man and woman got married. After the wedding, the couple went to a hotel. On the first night, the groom went to the bathroom and was in there for ages.

"What's taking you so long?" asked the bride.

"I'm brushing my teeth," replied the groom.

"It doesn't take that long to brush your teeth," said the bride.

"I'm brushing yours too," answered the groom.

CROSS YOUR LEGS

A middle-aged woman goes to the bar on a cruise ship and orders a whisky with two drops of water. As the bartender gives her the drink, she says, "I'm on this cruise to celebrate my birthday and it's today."

The bartender says, "Well, since it's your birthday, I'll buy you a drink. In fact, this one is on me."

As the woman finishes her drink, the man to her left says, "I would like to buy you a drink, too."

The birthday gal replies, "Thank you. Bartender, I want a whisky with two drops of water."

"Coming right up," says the bartender.

As she finishes that drink, the young woman to her right says, "I would like to buy you one, too."

The lady responds, "Thank you. Bartender, I want another whisky with two drops of water."

"Coming right up," the bartender says. As he gives her the beverage, he asks, "Ma'am, I'm dying to know. Why the whisky with only two drops of water?"

The lady replies, "Young man, when you're my age, you've learned how to hold your alcohol. Holding your water, however, is a whole other problem."

SEVENTY-FIVE AGAIN!

One day in 1994, the actor and comedian Victor Borge announced, "I'm celebrating my seventy-fifth birthday, which is sort of embarrassing, because I'm eighty-five."

A QUESTION OF PATERNITY

A couple are having an intimate meal to celebrate their fiftieth wedding anniversary.

The man leans forward and softly says to his wife, "Dear, there is something that I must ask you. It has always troubled me that our ninth child never looked quite like the rest of our brood. Now, I want to assure you that these fifty years have been the most wonderful experience, and your answer cannot take that away. But I must know, did he have a different father?"

The wife drops her head in shame, unable to look her husband straight in the eye. She pauses for a moment, then she replies, "Yes. Yes he did."

The man is shaken. The truth of what his wife is admitting hits him very hard.

With a lump in his throat, he asks, "Who? Who was he? Who was the father?"

Again, the woman hangs her head, saying nothing at first, as she tries to muster the courage to tell her husband the truth.

Then, finally, she says, "You."

DRINK UP

Alfred Lord Tennyson, who was Britain's Poet Laureate between the years 1850 and 1892, was renowned for his absent-mindedness, particularly as he grew older, and so it was one evening when he was entertaining the actor Henry Irving at dinner.

After the meal, the two men began to share a decanter of port. Although Irving was given one glass of the beverage, the butler then placed the rest of the bottle in front of Tennyson, who proceeded to refill his own glass, but not Irving's, until the whole bottle was finished.

Tennyson then asked the butler to bring a second bottle to the table. Again Irving's glass was filled once, but thereafter Tennyson drank the rest of the bottle himself.

The following morning, Irving found Tennyson standing by his bed. "Ah," said the Poet Laureate, "but pray, Mr. Irving, do you always drink two bottles of port after dinner?"

BAD GOLF DAY

A foursome of golfers hit the course with waning enthusiasm for the game.

"These hills are getting steeper as the years go by," one moaned.

"These fairways seem to be getting longer too," said one of the others, with a sigh.

"The sand traps are bigger than I remember them," moaned the third.

After hearing enough from his friends, the oldest and the wisest of the four of them piped up, "Just be thankful we're still on the right side of the grass!"

NINETY-NINE NOT OUT

On being given a huge chocolate birthday cake with ninety-nine candles on top of it, pensioner Edith Anne Drima looked more than a little put out.

"Don't you like it?" asked one of her nurses, concerned.

"It's not a matter of not liking it," replied Edith sharply. "If I try to blow all those candles out, I'm going to have a heart attack!"

BIRTHDAY GREETINGS

The older people get, often the more obstreperous and curmudgeonly they become, as was the case with Sir Thomas Beecham, who, on the occasion of his seventieth birthday, was given a celebratory dinner, during which telegrams and congratulations came in from all over—many from the world's greatest musicians and composers.

Even so, according to legend, Beecham was heard to mutter, "What, nothing from Mozart?"

A WIFE'S REVENGE

"Look at me," an arrogant gentleman boasted to his guests at his birthday bash. "I've aged like a fine, old, carefully stored wine."

"I certainly have to agree with that," piped up his obviously long-suffering spouse. "Henry's cork's been stationary for years."

AT THE WEDDING

At a family wedding, the mother of the bride was determined to keep her eyes bone dry so as not to smudge her delicately applied mascara. She was doing well—until the point in the service when she glanced over at her own mother, who was sitting next to her father.

As she watched the old couple together, her mother reached out to her father, who was at this stage in his life confined to a wheelchair and somewhat incapacitated, and softly stroked his hand. It was such a loving gesture that their daughter found tears running down her cheeks, and she was overcome at last.

After the ceremony, she made her way across the church to where her parents were sitting.

"Mother," she scolded affectionately, "it's your fault that I have panda eyes right now. I was holding it together until I saw you reach out for Dad. That just set me off. On this special day, it's wonderful to see the two of you still so much in love."

Her mother gave an amused snort. "I'm sorry to ruin your moment, my dear," she said bluntly, "but I was just checking to see if he was still alive."

HAPPY 40ᵀᴴ BIRTHDAY

My friend and I were celebrating our 40th birthdays the same year. As a gag gift, I gave her a CD by the band UB40.

For my birthday, she retaliated with a CD as well. The group? U2.

—Mona Turrell

A VERY SPECIAL DELIVERY

According to *The Times* of London, getting old can be a very confusing time—particularly when your friends send you presents. At least, this was the case for pensioner Fred Harrop.

The paper reported that opera aficionado Harrop was taken aback to receive a book of pornographic images as a birthday gift from chums. In an administrative error, Amazon.com had sent him *Literate Smut*, containing thirty-five sex photographs, rather than the volume his friends had ordered—*Backstage at the Opera with Cecilia Bartoli.*

Amazon apologized right away for the mistake, and later for the subsequent comment from a company spokesman, who told Harrop's friends: "If you think Mr. Harrop was disappointed, imagine how the guy who got the opera book felt."

IT'S FUNNY BECAUSE IT'S TRUE

On my birthday I got a really funny card from a friend. It joked about how our bodies might be getting older, but our minds were still "tarp as shacks."

I wanted to thank the friend who sent the card, but I couldn't. She forgot to sign it.

—Meris M. Mack

PACK YOUR BAGS

An excited woman called her husband at work. "I won the lottery!" she exclaimed. "Pack your clothes!"

"Great!" he replied. "Summer or winter clothes?"

"All of them—I want you out of the house by six!"

—Ashley Cooper in Charleston, S.C., *News and Courier*

9

Vanity Not So Fair

MORE SIGNS YOU'RE OVER THE HILL...

According to radio announcer Colin Slater, there are a few more signs you're over the hill:

- You hang your clothes on padded coat hangers.

- You go supermarket shopping in the evening to pick up marked-down bargains.

- You save the hearing-aid flyer that falls out of the newspaper supplement.

- You try to get electrical gadgets repaired when they go wrong.

- You store up the free little packets of sugar from cafés.

- You have worn a knitted swimsuit.

- When you watch black-and-white films, you spend the whole time pointing at the screen going, "He's dead... She's dead..."

GOOD NEWS, BAD NEWS

"My grandma told me, 'The good news is, after menopause the hair on your legs gets really thin and you don't have to shave any more. Which is great because it means you have more time to work on your new moustache.'"

—Karen Huber

CUTTING-EDGE FASHION

Elizabeth K., a Dutch fashion designer, was very excited when she was given a once-in-a-lifetime opportunity to take part in a prestigious New York fashion show at the Guggenheim Museum.

She worked for weeks on her collection, perfecting her designs. Then, because she didn't trust anyone else to make them, she did all the sewing herself. Day after day she sat in her studio, creating stunning dresses and skirts, stitching feathers and sequins on to the clothes by hand until, come the night of the show, the models climbed into the garments. In order that there was no VPL (visible panty line), Elizabeth K. insisted no underwear be worn.

As the music began, the models all started to parade down the catwalk, strutting their funky stuff. Suddenly, the audience began wolf-whistling and clapping. Elizabeth was pleased, but also a little disconcerted.

Then she realized what she'd done. In her desperation to get the collection finished on time, she'd forgotten to sew any linings into the garments. With the catwalk backlighting, *everything* was revealed. Needless to say, the show was a great success—although it took the models some time to appreciate exactly what it was that everyone was applauding.

SOUR CREAM

You definitely know you're over the hill when your children point out your shortcomings. Take, for example, the following anecdote from *Pass the Port* by Christian Brann.

"While watching her mother put some face cream on, a little girl was overheard asking, 'Mommy, is that the cream they show on the television that makes you beautiful?'

"The mother replied that it was, only for her daughter to say, 'It doesn't work very well, does it?'"

Ouch!

LOOKING GOOD

Sheila is standing in front of her full-length mirror, taking a long, hard look at herself.

"You know, Steve," she remarks. "I stare into this mirror and I see an ancient creature. My face is all creased and tired, my skin is wrinkled, and my eyes have more bags than Paris Hilton on a transatlantic flight. My arms and legs are as flabby as jelly, and my bottom looks like several deflated, popped balloons. Observe my boobs—they droop so much that they hang to my waist. My body has just gone to pot."

She turns to face her husband and says, "Dear, please tell me just one good thing about my body so that I can feel a bit better about myself."

Steve studies Sheila critically for a moment and then says in a gentle, thoughtful voice, "Well, there's nothing wrong with your eyesight."

HAIR TODAY...

If menopause is a sign that women are over the hill, surely it follows that baldness is a sign that men aren't quite the youthful creatures they used to be.

Being "follically challenged" is something that the eminent British philosopher Thomas Hobbes knew all about. In his eighties, Hobbes was almost completely bald, but he wouldn't wear a hat, claiming he never suffered from head colds.

Instead, the biggest problem "was to keep flies from pitching on the baldness."

...GONE TOMORROW

Or how about this observation from British comic Dave Barry on how those men who try to cover up their baldness only show themselves to be more over the hill than most?

"The method preferred by most balding men for making themselves look silly is called the comb-over, which is when the man grows the hair on one side of his head very long and combs it across the bald area, creating an effect that looks from the top like an egg in the grasp of a large tropical spider."

PRIORITIES

A woman paused in the middle of the street on a very blustery day, using both hands to hold on to her hat as a strong gust of wind blew her dress up around her waist.

A dignified gentleman came up to her and said, "Ma'am, you should be ashamed of yourself, letting your skirt blow around your middle, being indecent, while both hands hold your hat."

She said, "Look, mister, everything down there is as old as I am. This hat is brand new!"

LETTING YOURSELF GO

Women definitely know they are over the hill when they spend more and more hours each week at the beauty salon, trying to stave off old age.

For example, the American novelist and screenwriter Nora Ephron writes: "I am only about eight hours a week away from looking like a bag lady, with the frizzled, flyaway gray hair I would probably have if I stopped dying mine; with a pot belly I would definitely develop if I ate just half of what I think about eating every day; with the dirty nails and chapped lips and moustache and bushy eyebrows that would be my destiny if I ever spent two weeks on a desert island."

HAIR WE GO

In his wonderful tome *Braude's Handbook of Stories for Toastmasters and Speakers*, Jacob Braude relates many wonderful stories and quotes, but one of my favorites is this very silly joke.

"Can you give me a prescription for my hair?"asked the balding patient of his doctor. "It worries me."

"Don't worry, old man," said the specialist, "it'll all come out all right."

THE UNDERWEAR DEBATE

If you want to know whether you're over the hill or not, ask yourself this: does the underwear you buy for yourself disappoint you to the extent that you would write to the manufacturer or to a newspaper to complain about it? If the answer is "yes," then I'm afraid you're definitely on your way to senility. After all, aren't there more important things to be worrying about?

Not according to broadcaster and journalist Jeremy Paxman, who, in a private email (which was later leaked to the press) to Stuart Rose, head of Marks & Spencer, laid bare some issues he had with M&S underwear:

> Like very large numbers of men in this country, I have always bought my socks and pants in Marks and Sparks. I've noticed that something very troubling has happened. There's no other way to put this. Their pants no longer provide adequate support.
>
> When I've discussed this with friends and acquaintances, it has revealed widespread gusset anxiety.
>
> The other thing is socks. Even among those of us who clip our toenails very rigorously, they appear to be wearing out much more quickly on the big toe.
>
> Also, they are no longer ribbed around the top, which means they do not stay up in the way they used to. These are matters of great concern to the men in Britain.

Nor, it seems, is Mr. Paxman alone in his inability to come to terms with modern underwear. Take, for instance, the following rant by Lindsay Keir Wise, which appeared in *The Oldie* magazine in April 2008:

> I am sure that I speak for others in what is a very sensitive matter. The subject of my dissatisfaction is men's underpants […] When donning pants, one must ascertain (a) which is the inside and which is the outside and (b) which is the front and which is the back. In doing this, one is guided by the label at the back of the garment […]
>
> In the cause of sartorial advancement, prompted no doubt by the endorsement of a Beckham or Britney, pants manufacturers have taken to applying the label, hitherto the mark of orientation, not to the inside back but to the *outside front!* This intervention has disturbed the even tenor of my ways: I have not only found my underpants are inside out, but—if called to a public facility—that the exit hole is at the back…

REUNIONS

My 20th high-school class reunion was held at a hotel on the same night that another school's tenth-year reunion was taking place. While my friends and I were in the rest room talking, some unfamiliar women entered.

After their stares became uncomfortable, we turned toward them. One of the women said, "Don't mind us. We just wanted to see how we'd look in another ten years."

—Sondra Olivieri

REALITY CHECK

When a woman I know turned 99 years old, I went to her birthday party and took some photos. A few days later, I brought the whole batch of prints to her so she could choose her favorite.

"Good Lord," she said as she was flipping through them, "I look like I'm a hundred."

—Helen B. Marrow

LETTING GO

It's all right letting yourself go, as long as you can let yourself back.

—Mick Jagger

NOT LOOKING GOOD

A woman accompanied her husband when he went for his annual checkup. While the patient was getting dressed, the doctor came out and said to the wife, "I don't like the way he looks."

"Neither do I," she said. "But he's handy around the house."

—Merritt K. Freeman in *Y. B. News*

HARMONY IN NATURE

Overheard: "Marriage is nature's way of keeping people from fighting with strangers."

—Alan King

AN EASY DIET

Heard about the new diet? You eat whatever you want whenever you want, and as much as you want. You don't lose any weight, but it's really easy to stick to.

—George J. Tricker

GET IN SHAPE

Comic J. Scott Homan said he'd been trying to get in shape doing 20 sit-ups each morning. "That may not sound like a lot, but you can only hit that snooze alarm so many times."

—Atlanta *Journal-Constitution*

WHY DON'T YOU?

A couple walking in the park noticed a young man and woman sitting on a bench, passionately kissing.

"Why don't you do that?" said the wife.

"Honey," replied her husband, "I don't even know that woman!"

—Gary R. Handley

10

Frankly, My Dear

YOU KNOW YOU'RE OVER THE HILL WHEN...

- Your idea of weight lifting is standing up.

- An "all-nighter" means not getting up to use the bathroom.

- You look for your glasses for an hour... and then find that they were on top of your head all the time.

- You're more attractive standing on your head.

- Your wife believes your excuses for getting home late.
  —Basil Ransome-Davies

- The pharmacist has become your new best friend.

- It takes longer to rest than it did to get tired.

- You no longer think of speed limits as a challenge.

- Your knees buckle, but your belt won't.

- Your idea of a night out is sitting on the patio.

- There's no question in your mind that there's no question in your mind.

WRONG END OF THE STICK

Lady Constance Milligan was making some final arrangements for a large party she was going to throw that evening.

"Betty," she said to her loyal housekeeper, "for the first twenty minutes, I would like it if you'd stand at the drawing-room door and call the guests' names as they arrive."

Betty's face glowed with pleasure. "Thank you, madam," she replied. "I've been wanting to do that to your friends for the past thirty years."

IT'S EASY TO FORGET WHAT WE'VE FORGOTTEN

Forgetfulness is definitely one of the first signs of being over the hill, as the following anecdote, which first appeared in *Conversation, Please* by Loren Carroll, reveals.

A young lady who had called in on writer Agnes Repplier got ready to go, put on her hat and coat, put her hands in her muff, took them out, picked up a parcel, laid it down, shifted from one foot to another and then said, "There was something I meant to say, but I've forgotten."

"Perhaps, my dear," Miss Repplier replied, "it was goodbye."

AUTOMATICALLY

What an automated society we live in. Have you ever noticed that when a traffic signal turns green, it automatically activates the horn of the car behind you?

—Robert Orben in *The American Legion Magazine*

GETTING YOUR OWN BACK

A middle-aged woman is in her birthday suit, trampolining enthusiastically on her bed, giggling and humming with wild abandon. Her husband walks into the room. He watches her a while, then remarks, "You look absurd! What on earth do you think you're doing?"

She announces, "I just had a medical exam and my doctor says I have the breasts of an eighteen-year-old." She starts throwing herself about the bed again, trilling songs for all she's worth.

He snorts, "Yeah, right. And what did he say about your ass?"

"Your name never came up," she retorts.

OH CAROL!

According to an anecdote told by Truman Capote in *Answered Prayers* (1986), the Hollywood actor Walter Matthau was once at a party with his wife Carol, when she overheard him talking to an elderly woman who, as Carol described her, was "mutton dressed as lamb."

Apparently, Walter was then overheard asking, "How old are you?" At which point, Carol butted in and said, "Why don't you saw off her legs and count the rings?"

SPEAK YOUR MIND

A forthright connoisseur of culture, whose increasing years had made her increasingly frank, was among a group looking at an art exhibition in a newly opened gallery. Suddenly, one contemporary painting caught her eye.

"What on earth," she inquired of the artist standing nearby, "is that?"

He smiled condescendingly. "That, my dear lady, is supposed to be a cow and its calf."

"Well, then," snapped the woman in reply, "why isn't it?"

ANOTHER CASE OF
FOOT-IN-MOUTH DISEASE

One day, Mrs. Cholmondely was entertaining at home and employed a famous violinist to entertain her guests. When the musician had finished his recital, everyone crowded around him.

"I must be honest," said one of the guests, "I'm afraid I thought your performance was awful."

Quickly, Mrs. Cholmondely interrupted: "Oh don't pay any attention to him. He hasn't the slightest idea what he's talking about. He only repeats what he hears everyone else saying!"

NOTHING LIKE A GOOD MEMORY

Being old is sometimes a fantastic disguise. People assume that you're frail and decrepit, that your mind is full of holes and your bladder full of urine. But, on occasion, a razor-sharp wit nestles beneath the chapped tongue, and a fine brain resides in the gray-haired head.

A small-town prosecuting attorney called his first witness to the stand in a trial—a grandmotherly woman who had long been a respected member of the local community. He approached her and asked, "Mrs. Pickford, do you know me?"

She responded, "Why, yes, I do know you, Mr. Moore. I've known you since you were a child. And frankly, you've been a big disappointment to me. You lie, you cheat on your girlfriend, you manipulate people and talk about them behind their backs. You think you're a big shot when you haven't the brains to realize you will never amount to anything more than a two-bit paper pusher. Yes, I know you."

The lawyer was stunned. Not knowing what else to do, he pointed across the room and asked, "Mrs. Pickford, do you know the defense attorney?"

She again replied, "Why, yes, I do. I've known Mr. Pearce since he was a youngster, too. I used to babysit him for his parents. And he, too, has been a real disappointment to me. He's lazy, prejudiced, he has a gambling problem. The man can't build a good relationship with anyone and his estate is one of the shoddiest in the entire neighborhood. Yes, I know him."

At this point, the judge rapped the courtroom to silence and called both counselors to the bench. In a very quiet voice, he said with menace, "If either of you asks her if she knows me, you'll be in jail for contempt before you can draw breath!"

SNOOZING

It's hard to know sometimes exactly who is the one who's over the hill, but I think in this next anecdote the clergyman is the one left with most egg on his face...

After a very long and rather tedious Sunday service at her local church, a middle-aged woman approached the minister and shook his hand.

"Reverend," she exclaimed, "I do apologize for dozing off during your sermon.

"But," she added succinctly, "I want you to know I didn't miss a thing."

FEISTY

Feisty to the end, transcendental philosopher Henry David Thoreau was absolute proof that the older you grow, the more belligerent you become.

Toward his twilight years, he was asked if he'd like to make his peace with God.

"I did not know that we had ever quarreled," he replied frostily.

HERE WE GO AGAIN

Some Canadians were traveling by tour bus through Holland. They stopped at a cheese farm, where a young guide led them through the process of cheese making, explaining that goat's milk was used.

She showed the group a hillside, on which many goats were grazing. "These," she explained "are the older goats put out to pasture when they no longer produce."

She then asked, "What do you do in Canada with your old goats?"

A sprightly old gentleman answered, "They send us on coach tours!"

WE ALL FALL DOWN

Chat-show host Jay Leno clearly has all his mental faculties intact. The quick-witted presenter once remarked: "The University of Nebraska says that elderly people that drink beer or wine at least four times a week have the highest bone density. They need it—they're the ones falling down most."

THE LETTERS PAGE

Another symptom of growing old is our predilection for writing to national newspapers, complaining about something, writing to complain about people who complain, or simply passing on words of wisdom gained from many years of experience.

This letter to *The Oldie* is a veritable gem from a savvy senior.

> What's all the fuss about being asked one's date of birth? The answer is easy—just do as I do and lie. As far as I know, there's no law that says you can't pretend to be a forgetful old bag. Live up to the expectations of John Q. Public about elderly dottiness when it suits you.
>
> —Margaret Love (*The Oldie*, April 2008)

DO YOU REMEMBER ME?

According to *Braude's Handbook,* Winston Churchill had the perfect riposte for those indiscreet enough to ask, "Do you remember me?"

Sir Winston always replied, "Why should I?"

HOW UNCOOL

Hip-hop rapper and actor L.L. Cool J. was once asked in an interview if he still expected to be rapping in thirty years' time.

"We'll see what Vegas is paying," he said. "I'll be rapping about denture cream, Preparation H. My pants will still be sagging—but it'll be from Depends!"

LOVELY LONGEVITY

The pastor's message was "Forgive Your Enemies."

He asked, "How many of you have forgiven your enemies?" About half his parishioners held up their hands.

He repeated the question; now about 70 percent of the congregation answered his query in the affirmative. One more time, he questioned his flock—now all raised their hands, except for one elderly lady.

"Mrs. Barrow, are you not willing to forgive your enemies?" the pastor asked, with faint disapproval.

"I don't have any," she responded proudly.

"Mrs. Barrow, that is very uncommon. How old are you?"

"Eighty-seven," she replied.

"Mrs. Barrow, would you please come forward and explain to us all how a person cannot have an enemy in the world."

The little angelic lady tottered down the aisle and announced, "It's easy. I just outlived those bitches."

ROCK STAR LIFE

In January 2003, rock groups KISS and Aerosmith announced that they were going to embark on a world tour together during the forthcoming summer. "They could call it the Tongue and Lips Tour," *Salon*'s Amy Reiter suggested.

Sometime later, it was pointed out that both groups had played together more than thirty years earlier.

"On the other hand," Reiter then joked, "maybe they should call it the Dentures and Bifocals Tour."

HOME TRUTHS

Late Night show host Conan O'Brien was once asked what his program's time slot (12:35 a.m.) revealed about his audience.

"It means they're mostly prisoners, pimps, and embezzlers," Conan replied. "And a lot of college kids who've just discovered glue sniffing.

"If it's an older person, it means they probably need to take a medication late at night. They come up to me and say, 'I put a cream on my ass at 12:34 a.m., and then you come on!'"

DEFINE YOUR AGE

The art historian and novelist Anita Brookner, irritated by the constant speculation about her age which appeared in the press after she won the Booker Prize for Fiction with *Hotel du Lac* in 1984, wrote to *The Times* on November 5, 1984 to say, "I am forty-six, and have been for some past time."

EZRA POUND

As an old man, the poet Ezra Pound was a virtual recluse, but in *The Oxford Book of American Literary Anecdotes,* editor Donald Hall recounts the following story.

A young poet who was traveling in Italy knocked on Pound's door one day, never expecting the eminent poet to open the door himself. Seconds later, however, Pound appeared in the hallway in his dressing gown and slippers. "How are you, Mr. Pound?" asked the astonished young gentleman. Pound remained silent for quite some time as if pondering the question. Finally, he opened his mouth. "Senile," he said.

I AM *NOT* OVER THE HILL

After watching her son Cary Grant on television once, his mother, who was in her nineties, told him off for allowing his hair to go gray.

"It doesn't bother me," he replied, with good humor.

"Maybe not," said his mother, "But it bothers *me*. It makes me seem old."

PREMONITIONS

In 1906, Gertrude Stein had her portrait painted by Pablo Picasso, but it wasn't an easy affair. In fact, the collaboration was a long, arduous one and Stein was asked to sit no fewer than eighty times, after which Picasso declared that he could not "see" her any more and promptly left for Spain.

Some time later, however, apparently inspired by an exhibit of a particular piece of sculpture at the Louvre in Paris, Picasso completed the portrait and presented it to Gertrude, who immediately complained that she looked nothing like the figure he had portrayed.

"No," Picasso replied, then added, very unkindly, "but you will."

I CAN'T HANG ON ANY LONGER, DEAR

The actress Edith Evans was never anything if not direct. Such a quality has even greater liberty with one's increasing years.

During rehearsals for what was proving to be a rather melodramatic play, Evans once said to a much younger fellow actress: "I'm a very old lady. I may die during one of your pauses."

11

And
So It Goes...

YOU KNOW YOU'RE OVER THE HILL WHEN...

- Your computer has more memory than you do.

- You realize caution is the only thing you care to exercise.

- You read more and remember less.

- You and your other half wear coordinated outfits.

- Your family discusses you as though you're not in the room.

- Everyone is happy to give you a ride because they don't want you behind the wheel.

- Your body becomes shorter, but your stories become longer.

- You fib about your grandchildren's ages.

THE IMPORTANCE OF BEING IMPORTANT

The following extract from D. J. Enright's *Play Resumed* sums up perfectly that moment when you definitely know you are over the hill.

> The contents of this envelope are important and require your immediate attention. To begin with, opening the envelope is a major undertaking, and wouldn't be easy if you were in full possession of your fingers. And then, though you labor to make them so, the contents are not in the least important to you, nor you to them. Why is everything *important* these days? Because so many things are of no consequence.

PRESENCE OF OLD AGE

A grandmother was giving directions to her grandson, who was coming to visit her with his wife and kids.

"You come to the front door of the apartment block. I am in apartment 16A. There is a big panel at the door. With your elbow, push button 16A. I will buzz you in. Come inside, the elevator is on the right. Get in, and with your elbow hit 16. When you get out, I am on the left. With your elbow, hit my doorbell."

"Grandma, that sounds easy," replied the grandson, "but I don't understand why I'm hitting all these buttons with my elbow."

To which she answered, "You're coming empty-handed?"

BANANAS!

You definitely know you're over the hill when your husband acts like this...

"As I stripped off my sweatshirt at the breakfast table one warm morning, my T-shirt started to come off too. My husband let out a low whistle. I took it as a compliment—until he said, from behind his newspaper, 'Can you believe the price of bananas?'"

YOU'RE NEXT!

Juliet Walsh, aged seventy-six, never tired of going to weddings, during which her favorite pastime was nudging all the twenty-year-olds and telling them, "You're next."

But Juliet stopped doing this when someone said the exact same thing to her—only this time, she was at a funeral!

THREE LETTERS OF LOVE

Three sons grew up, left home, went out on their own and prospered. Meeting up for dinner one night, they discussed the presents they'd given their dear mother for her recent birthday.

The first son said, "I constructed a mansion for our mother."

The second said, "I sent her a BMW with a chauffeur."

The third smiled and said, "I've got you both beat. You know how Mom enjoys the Bible? Well, we all know that she can't see too well any more to read it herself. So I bought her a parrot that can recite the entire Bible. It took sixteen

nuns in a remote convent eleven years to teach him. I had to pledge to contribute $300,000 a year for a whole decade, but it was worth it. Mom just has to name the chapter and verse, and the parrot will recite it.'

Soon after, the mother penned her letters of thanks and posted them to her children.

"Roger," she wrote to the first son, "the mansion you built is so huge. I live in only two rooms, but I have to maintain the entire building."

"Rory," she wrote to the second son, "I am too frail to travel. I stay home all the time, so I never use the BMW. And the chauffeur is so rude!"

"Dearest Randall," she wrote to her third son, "you were the only son to have the good sense to know what your mother likes. That chicken was delicious."

SPLASHING AROUND

According to his wife, novelist G. K. Chesterton was renowned for having odd lapses of memory—none more so than on one particular day when he had gone to take a bath. Standing outside the bathroom door, she heard him get out of the tub, after which there was a long interval and then a loud splashing noise.

Apparently, Chesterton had forgotten that he'd already bathed and had sat back in the bath again.

On realizing his error, his wife then heard him exclaim: "Damn, I've been here before!"

HOW TO MAKE YOUR CHILDREN FEEL GUILTY

One weekend, a woman decided to call her father in California because it had been quite some time since they had chatted.

The woman asked her father, "How are you doing?"

"Not too good," he said. "I've been very weak."

'Pop, why are you so weak?' the daughter asked.

He said, "Because I haven't eaten anything in thirty-eight days."

The daughter then asked, "How come you haven't eaten in thirty-eight days?"

"Because I didn't want my mouth to be filled with food when you called," he replied.

FORGOTTEN STORIES

Sebastian and Fred, who were both in their early fifties, were sitting on a park bench, enjoying the sunshine and catching up with one another.

"So, Seb, what's new with you?" asked Fred.

Seb looked a little bit troubled. "To be honest," he replied, "I had a really great story I wanted to tell you, but I've already forgotten it."

"Oh," said Fred, "well, if it's about 'forgotten stories,' I have a better one to tell you than that ... if only I could remember it!"

BY MY CALCULATIONS

Three befuddled men are at their local hospital for a test. The doctor asks the first man, "What is three times three?"

"560," is his reply.

The doctor is exasperated, but he has hope for the other patients. He says to the second man, "It's your turn. What is three times three?"

"Saturday," replies the second man.

The doctor tuts, and tells the third man, "OK, your turn. What's three times three?"

"Nine," responds the third man.

"Fantastic!" exclaims the doctor. "Well done! How did you get that?"

"Simple," he replies, "just subtract 560 from Saturday."

ALWAYS LOOK ON THE BRIGHT SIDE

The best thing about being senile is that you can hide your own Easter eggs and be surprised by the Christmas presents you've bought yourself.

ECONOMICS

Rachel had just become a widow and needed to put an obituary in the local paper about her late husband, Sam. She called the newspaper and asked, "How much does it cost to put an obituary in the paper?"

"The cost is 60 cents per word," replied the editor.

Rachel said, "Fine. Please print: 'Sam died.'"

The astonished editor explained that there was an eight-word minimum charge. Rachel thought for a moment, then said, "OK, please print: 'Sam died. 1983 pick-up truck now for sale.'"

TOOTHLESS

Losing one's teeth is no laughing matter. Regrettably, the older one gets, the more likely it is to occur.

The writer James Stern recalled that he and W. H. Auden used to 'have a race as to which of us would be the first to

lose all his teeth. I forget who won, but it was a near thing. He had just acquired his first set [of dentures] when—at a Boston tea party given in his honor by a group of elderly ladies—the hostess asked him to extinguish the flame under the silver kettle. Auden, now forty-five and far from thinking, filled his lungs to capacity. And blew!

"'My dear, the *din*!' exclaimed Auden later. 'My uppers went crashing into my neighbor's empty teacup!'"

HIS BARK IS WORSE THAN HIS BITE

According to a news item posted on a German website, a mature shoplifter in Braunschweig, Germany tried to evade arrest by biting two security guards.

However, pensioner Gustav Ernegger had forgotten to put in his dentures—as a result of which, all he was able to leave was a gummy red mark.

Said police spokesman Gunther Brauner: "He tried to bite the officer several times, but had forgotten to put his false teeth in and so was unable to cause him any harm."

CUP OF TEA?

Adam Smith, author of *The Wealth of Nations*, must have felt he was old before his time when he once placed a slice of bread and butter into a teapot instead of tea leaves and, having poured in boiling water and tasted the brew, declared it the worst cup of tea he had ever had the displeasure of drinking.

THE MARCH OF TIME

Long-windedness—or so I've been told by various youngsters—is yet another sign that you are fast becoming over the hill. Sir Josiah Stamp obviously knew this only too well for, while making a speech to the Chicago Club, he expressed concern that he was talking for too long and consequently boring his audience.

"I wouldn't like to be in the position of the parson," he explained, "who in the midst of an interminable sermon, suddenly stopped to chide: 'You know, I don't mind a bit having you look at your watches to see what time it is, but it really annoys me when you put them up to your ears to see if they are still running.'"

BAD NIGHTGOWN DAY

Searching in the mall for a comfy cotton nightgown, Hannah decided to try her luck in a shop renowned for its sexy lingerie, without much hope of finding something suitable.

However, to her delight, she found the perfect nightdress. Moreover, while waiting in line to purchase her selection, she noticed a young woman behind her holding the exact same nightie.

This proved what she had long suspected: despite being in her forties, she had kept up more than adequately with current fashions.

"I see we have the same taste," she said, somewhat proudly, to the teenager behind her.

"Yes," the young woman replied. "I'm getting this for my grandma."

YOU *CAN* BE TOO CAREFUL

After avoiding ATM machines for years because of his fears of identity fraud, a man in Germany finally plucked up the courage to use one—and was immediately arrested.

The forty-year-old spent so long checking that the machine was safe—inspecting it for hidden CCTV cameras and even donning a pair of surgical gloves so that he wouldn't leave fingerprints when he entered his PIN—that police picked him up for acting suspiciously.

THE POLITICS OF OLD AGE

Two retired schoolteachers were vacationing with their wives at a villa in the South of France. They were sitting on the patio one warm evening, watching the sun set and sipping cool aperitifs.

The sociology teacher asked his friend, "Have you read Marx?"

To which his colleague replied, "Yes and I think it's these damned wicker chairs."

WHO ARE YOU TALKING ABOUT?

Three women were sitting side by side in a noisy café one afternoon, reminiscing.

The first recalled shopping at the grocery store in her early married life, and demonstrated with her hands the length and thickness of a cucumber that she could buy for a fraction of today's prices.

The second woman nodded, adding that onions used to be much bigger. She demonstrated the size of the two big onions she used to pick up on her weekly shopping trip.

Then the woman lady chipped in with: "I can't hear a word you're saying, but I remember the guy you're talking about."

MARITAL MATH

One day, a frustrated wife told her close friend Jilly her definition of retirement: "Twice as much husband on half as much pay."

MODERN TECHNOLOGY

Yet another sign of impending old age is when technology starts to leave you behind, something that *Private Eye* editor Ian Hislop seems to know all about.

"People tell me that blogs are the future. Oh well, maybe I won't be part of it. I've re-designed the website of *Private Eye* so that when you go on, there's a big message that flashes up, which says: 'Go and buy the magazine.'"

OVER AND DONE WITH?

"Power? It has come to me too late. There were days when, on waking, I felt I could move dynasties [...]; but that has passed away."

—Benjamin Disraeli

PUZZLED

A man summons his wife and says: "Look, I've put this cityscape jigsaw puzzle together in six days!"

The wife asks: "What's so great about you putting a puzzle together in six days?"

"Well, the box says 4–7 years!" replies the man.

GETTING WHAT YOU DESERVE

"I really don't deserve this," Jack Benny once remarked, while accepting an award. "But I have arthritis and I don't deserve that either."

HOME, JAMES!

Nineteenth-century Austrian artist Max Schödel was blatantly over the hill when he flagged down a taxi in his capital city Vienna one morning.

According to several stories about the incident, the taxi driver, naturally, asked Schödel where he wanted to go.

Schödel had to think for a while before answering, "Number six."

That was all he could recall of the address, but he is said to have added, "just keep driving and I'll give you the street name when I remember it."

DON'T WORRY

An elderly woman was nervous about making her first flight in an airplane, so before takeoff she went to speak to the captain about her fears.

"You will bring me down safely, won't you?" she anxiously inquired.

"Don't worry, madam," was his friendly reply. "I haven't left anyone up there yet."

—Colleen Burger

STEP AWAY FROM THE CAR

Jokes are often made about one's driving skills diminishing as one gets older. Whatever the truth of the claim, I think we'd all agree that having one car accident is bad enough, but when you have four in the space of one month—as happened to comedian George Burns – a line really has to be drawn.

After the accidents, Burns decided to employ a driver to take him around, though he still wouldn't admit that his driving was dangerous. He was at pains to point out, only three of those accidents had been his fault!

WILL YOU MARRY ME?

She answered the phone to hear a repentant voice. "I'm sorry, darling," he said. "I have thought things over and you can have the Rolls-Royce as a wedding present, we will move to the Gold Coast, and your mother can stay with us. Now will you marry me?"

"Of course I will," she said. "And who is this speaking?"

—The Rotarian

BARN CONVERSION

Similarly silly is the anecdote about the late, great actress Edith Evans, who on hearing that some people "were living in Barnes" is supposed to have retorted, "What? Couldn't they afford a house?"

A SLAP ON THE FACE

An 85-year-old widow went on a blind date with a 90-year-old man. When she returned to her daughter's house later that night, she seemed upset. "What happened, Mother?" the daughter asked.

"I had to slap his face three times!"

"You mean he got fresh?"

"No," she answered. "I thought he was dead!"

—Warren Holl

TILL DEATH DO YOU PART

A man fond of weddings was being married for a fourth time. The groom seemed very moved as he stood at the altar with his new bride, and as he stood dabbing his eyes after the ceremony, his concerned best man asked him why he was so emotional.

"Well," replied the groom, "it just occurred to me that this could be my last wedding."

—Berte Goderstad

BARN CONVERSION

Similarly silly is the anecdote about the late, great actress Edith Evans, who on hearing that some people "were living in Barnes" is supposed to have retorted, "What? Couldn't they afford a house?"

PERSONAL BIAS

Congratulating a friend after her son and daughter got married within a month of each other, a woman asked, "What kind of boy did your daughter marry?"

"Oh, he's wonderful," gushed the mother. "He lets her sleep late, wants her to go to the beauty parlor regularly, and insists on taking her out to dinner every night."

"That's nice," said the woman. "What about your son?"

"I'm not so happy about that," the mother sighed. "His wife sleeps late, spends all her time in the beauty parlor, and makes them eat take-out meals!"

—Sabeen

KEEPING SECRETS

I was talking with an elderly relative who had just celebrated his 55th wedding anniversary. "Are there any secrets between you two?" I asked. "Do you ever hide anything from each other?"

"Well, yes," replied the old man with a sly smile. "I have ten thousand dollars in a bank that Mary doesn't know about. And she has ten thousand in a bank that I don't know about."

—James A. Sanaker

SWAY TO THE MUSIC

Fans of '60s music, my 14-year-old daughter and her best friend got front-row tickets to a Peter, Paul and Mary concert. When they returned home, my daughter said, "During the show, we looked back and saw hundreds of little lights swaying to the music. At first we thought the people were holding up cigarette lighters. Then we realized that the lights were the reflections off all the eyeglasses in the audience."

—Tracy Flachsbarth

NATURAL RESOURCES

Discussing the environment with his friend, one man asked, "Which of our natural resources do you think will become exhausted first?"

"The taxpayer," answered the other.

—Winston K. Pendleton,
Complete Speaker's Galaxy of
Funny Stories, Jokes and Anecdotes

BANK IN TROUBLE

Overheard: "I think our bank is in trouble. I was about to complete a withdrawal at the ATM and the machine asked me if I wanted to go double or nothing."

—*The Rotarian*

BE PREPARED

The couple had reached an age where the wife thought it was time to start considering wills and funeral arrangements rather than be caught unprepared. Her husband, however, wasn't too interested in the topic.

"Would you rather be buried or cremated?" she asked him.

There was a pause, then he replied from behind his paper, "Surprise me."

—Jim Gibson in the Victoria, B.C., *Times-Colonist*

WHAT I WOULD GIVE

A grieving widow was discussing her late husband with a friend.

"My Albert was such a good man, and I miss him so. He provided well for me with that fifty-thousand-dollar insurance policy—but I would give a thousand of it just to have him back."

—*Farmer's Digest*

GO AHEAD

At a wedding reception, a priest and a rabbi met at the buffet table. "Go ahead," said the priest, "try one of these delicious ham sandwiches. Overlooking your divine rule just this once won't do you any harm."

"That I will do, dear sir," the rabbi replied, "on the day of your wedding!"

—Kim DuBois

HE ONLY SLEEPS

In Las Vegas a big-time gambler dies and a friend delivers the eulogy. "Tony isn't dead," the friend says. "He only sleeps."

A mourner in the back of the room jumps up. "I got a hundred bucks says he's dead!"

—Solutions for Seniors

12

Good-bye
and Amen

YOU KNOW YOU'RE OVER THE HILL WHEN...

- You can't take out a thirty-year mortgage.

- You become obsessed with the thermostat.
  —Jeff Foxworthy

- You go on a summer holiday and pack a sweater.
  —Denis Norden

- You start calling your offspring by the dog's name.

- You realize that a stamp today costs more than a picture show did when you were growing up.

- You put on two pounds eating an olive.

- Your short-term memory has been replaced by a notepad and pen... but you can't remember where you put them.

- You know all medical terms and burial sites.

- You have more fingers on your hands than real teeth in your mouth.
  —Rodney Dangerfield

- You go to the dictionary to look up a word, spend minutes locating it, then realize you're staring down at the word "dictionary."

- You still chase women, but only downhill.   —Bob Hope

- Your supply of brain cells is finally down to a size you can handle.

- Everything hurts and what doesn't hurt, doesn't work.

- The only thing you still retain is water.   —Alex Cole

- Your mind makes contracts your body can't keep.

PLAYING GOD

A doctor died and went to heaven, where he found a long line at St. Peter's gate. As was his custom, the doctor rushed to the front, but St. Peter told him to wait in line like everyone else. Muttering and looking at his watch, the doctor stood at the end of the line.

Moments later a white-haired man wearing a white coat and carrying a stethoscope and medical bag rushed up to the front of the line, waved to St. Peter, and was immediately admitted through the Pearly Gates.

"Hey!" the doctor shouted. "How come you let him through?"

"Oh," said St. Peter, "that's God. Sometimes he likes to play doctor."

—Patricia Thomas

CULTURAL DIFFERENCES

Shortly after my husband passed away, one of my daughter's Jewish friends approached her with a question. "Kate," he said, "I've never attended a Catholic wake before. What is the significance of the widow not wearing shoes?"

Kate replied, "My mom's feet hurt."

—Marie May

WAY TO GO

Death is one of life's certainties and, for those of a particular age, it holds something of a peculiar fascination. As we grow older, we start to wonder, rather morbidly, just how we might leave this earth.

So, when little Danny's pet hamster died, and a kindly neighbor helped him bury it in the garden, death was not far from the elderly neighbor's thoughts.

Placing his hand on the boy's shoulder, the man explained carefully that death comes to all creatures, man and beast, and that the hamster had lived a full life and received a proper burial, just as it should be.

"So, little boy, how would you like to die?" queried the man.

Danny pondered the question solemnly, and then replied: "I want to die sleeping like my grandfather, not screaming like the passengers in the car."

RECOGNIZE HIM?

You know you're over the hill when people speak only well of you...

A man died. A wonderful funeral was taking place, during which the preacher talked at length of the good traits of the deceased. The preacher went on about "what an honest man" and "what a loving husband and kind father" he was.

Finally, after hearing all of this praise, the widow leaned over and whispered to her youngest child, "Go up there and take a look in the coffin. See if that's your father in there."

BACK FROM THE DEAD

There can be no greater sign that you're over the hill than when your own acquaintances think you're dead. Take, for instance, the following story, which involves three formidable ladies of the stage.

One day, in Katherine Cornell's dressing room, Mrs. Leslie Carter and Mrs. Patrick Campbell greeted one another.

"I'm very honored," said Mrs. Campbell. She took hold of Mrs. Carter's hand and shook it, before turning to Katherine Cornell and, in a very loud voice, confided, "I thought she was dead."

HARD AS A ROCK

The Greek poet Aeschylus certainly knew the dangers of growing old, for it is said that his death came about when an eagle, who had captured a tortoise and needed a stone on which to break open the poor creature's shell, mistook Aeschylus's bald head for a rock ... and dropped the tortoise on it!

FUNEREAL MOMENTS

There can be no greater reminder that one is getting on in life than when one's thoughts begin turning to funeral arrangements.

A little before his death, the elderly and somewhat infirm Lord Chesterfield was accustomed to being taken out in his coach and horses. In fact, so infirm was he that the horses were usually made to go at no more than a walk.

One day, while engaged in this activity, a friend came up to Lord Chesterfield's carriage to congratulate the old man on still being able to get out and take the air.

"I thank you kindly, sir," said his lordship, "but I do not come out so much for the air, as for the benefit of rehearsing my funeral."

HEAVEN-SENT

Bob and Joe are two retired widowers, who reside close to each other and do occasional welfare checks on each other, when they remember.

One day, as he drinks his morning tea, Joe opens the local paper and turns to the Obituaries page. He gets the shock of his life when he sees his own obituary in the column.

He correctly surmises that it's simply a mistaken entry from the paper's database, premature and erroneous. The gaffe still rankles him, so he calls up Bob.

"Bob, are you up yet?"

Bob answers sleepily, "Yeah, but I'm only now eating my breakfast."

"Bob, open the newspaper to page 42."

"Why, what's in the paper?"

"Bob, get the paper and open it to page 42 now!"

"OK, OK, I've got the paper here. So what's on page 42?"

"Bob, open the damn paper to page 42."

"All right, don't be such a damn pain in the ass so early in the morning. What's on page 42 that's so important?"

"Bob, look at the bottom of column four."

"Why? What's that story on?"

"Bob, read the damn story on the bottom of the damn column."

"OK, OK, I'll start reading the damn column if you stop yelling in my ear!"

The paper rustles for a few seconds, then a long pause ensues.

Finally, Bob comes on the line quietly and fearfully. "So, Joe, where are you calling me from right now?"

SUICIDAL THOUGHTS

A mature widow is distraught after the death of her faithful spouse. She can't live without him and decides that the best way to do herself in is to stab herself in her pitifully broken heart. Still, she doesn't want to mess it up, so she calls a doctor to find out exactly where the heart is.

He tells her to put her first two fingers together, hold them horizontally and place the tip of the first finger just below her left nipple. The heart, he says, is immediately below the first knuckle on her second finger.

Later that day, the doctor is called to the Emergency Room to put thirteen stitches in the woman's left thigh.

YOU KNOW YOU'RE OVER THE HILL WHEN... YOU DIE ON THE JOB

John Entwistle, bass guitarist with The Who, died in 2002 while in bed with a stripper. Lead singer of the group, Roger Daltrey, commented that he'd miss his friend and fellow band member, but added:

"Ask any man what he would prefer: to live to a ripe old age and die alone, or to go out shagging your balls off with strippers in Vegas. Come on, let's be honest. It's not a death that any man should be ashamed of."

IN VERY BAD TASTE

A funeral service is being held for a woman who has just died. At the end of the ceremony, the pall-bearers are carrying the casket out of the church when they bump into a wall. They hear a quiet moan! They open the casket and

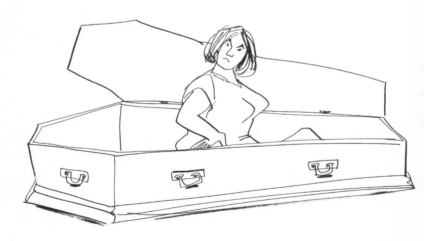

find that the woman is actually still alive. She lives for six more years, and then dies.

Once again, a service is held, and at the end of it, the pall-bearers are again carrying out the casket. As they near the door, the husband cries out: "Watch that wall!"

ONE FOOT IN THE GRAVE

In the latter part of his life, French composer Daniel Auber was one day attending a funeral service.

"I believe," he remarked to one of his fellow mourners, "that this is the last time I'll take part as an amateur."

DIRT NAP

Late one night, after an evening of drinking, Smitty took a shortcut through the graveyard and stumbled into a newly dug grave. He could not get out, so he lay at the bottom and fell asleep. Early next morning the old caretaker heard moans and groans coming from deep in the earth. He went over to investigate, saw the shivering figure at the bottom and demanded, "What's wrong with ya, that you're makin' all that noise?"

"Oh, I'm awful cold!" came the response.

"Well, it's no wonder," said the caretaker. "You've gone and kicked all the dirt off ya!"

—Debbie P. Wright

HEAVENLY MESSAGES

Two men have been best friends for years, and are a great comfort to each other in their dotage. Suddenly, one of them falls ill. His mate comes to visit him on his deathbed, and they're reminiscing about their long friendship, when the dying man's buddy asks, "Listen, when you die, do me a favor. I want to know if there's cricket in heaven."

The sick man replies, "We've been friends for decades; this I'll do for you." And then he dies.

A couple of days later, the surviving friend is sleeping when he hears his chum's voice. The voice says, "I've got some good news and some bad news. The good news is that there's cricket in heaven."

"What's the bad news?"

"You're bowling on Thursday."

REGRETS, I'VE HAD A FEW

Being over the hill often involves a great deal of introspection. As we age, we contemplate and review our lives more and more regularly.

On his deathbed, the actor Stanley Holloway (who played Eliza Doolittle's father in the film *My Fair Lady*) was asked whether he had any regrets.

Pausing to think about it, Holloway finally said, "Yes — the fact that I never got the Kipling cake commercials."

HELP!

In a panic, a traveler called down to the hotel's front desk soon after checking in. "Help!" he yelled. "I'm trapped inside my room!"

"What do you mean, trapped?"

"Well, I see three doors," the man explained. "The first opens to a closet, and the second to a bathroom. And the third door has a 'Do Not Disturb' sign hanging on it."

—Peter S. Greenberg, Los Angeles Times Syndicate

LIFE INSURANCE

Often, our spouses realize we're on our last legs long before we do.

One day, John ends up in hospital, having been run over by a ten-ton truck. His best friend Tom goes to see him every day, and every day John tells Tom, "My wife Katie visits here three times a day. She's so good to me. She brings me sweets and reads to me at the bedside."

Finally, Tom asks John what Katie is reading to him. "My life insurance policy, of course!"

GRAVEYARD HUMOR

There is no surer way to know that you're over the hill than when you're dead. On his gravestone, dramatist Eugene O'Neill had these rather sweet words inscribed:

> EUGENE O'NEILL
> There is something
> To be said
> For being dead